A MAGNUM FOR SCHNEIDER

In February 1967, a one-off television drama in the series *Armchair Theatre* introduced the surly, complex and ferociously downbeat character of David Callan – a professional hit-man working for a very dirty section of British Intelligence. As portrayed by the actor Edward Woodward, Callan was to become an iconic figure of espionage fiction, appearing in novels, a film and an immensely popular television series. This is the first of five novels written by Callan's creator, James Mitchell, featuring his human, but not necessarily pleasant hero.

A MAGNUM FOR SCHNEIDER

A MAGNUM FOR SCHNEIDER

by

James Mitchell

Magna Large Print Books
Long Preston, North Yorkshire,
BD23 4ND, England.

British Library Cataloguing in Publication Data.

Mitchell, James
    A magnum for Schneider.

    A catalogue record of this book is
    available from the British Library

    ISBN   978-0-7505-3959-3

First published in Great Britain in 1969

Cover illustration by arrangement with Ostara Publishing

Published in Large Print 2014 by arrangement with
Ostara Publishing

Magna Large Print is an imprint of Library Magna Books Ltd.

Printed and bound in Great Britain by
T.J. (International) Ltd., Cornwall, PL28 8RW

For Edward Woodward

CHAPTER ONE

The place hadn't changed. There was no reason to suppose it ever would. Once it had been a school, and the playground made a useful enough car-park. The building itself had the special kind of nastiness – red brick, green paint, mud-coloured corridors that never got enough light – that Callan remembered from his boyhood. There were classrooms and an assembly hall and the headmaster's room, all littered with broken desks and easel blackboards; there was an art room, a gym, a woodwork shop and a metalwork shop. But the place was silent now, always silent. No yelling at playtimes, no singing, no chanting of tables. Instead, there was a jumble of cars and vans in the playground, and a sign outside the main entrance: C. Hunter Ltd. Dealer in Scrap Metal. There were the closed-circuit television cameras as well, but you couldn't see them. You weren't supposed to. They saw you.

Callan walked in and rang the bell. The

9

man who answered it was everything a scrap metal dealer should be: gross, powerful, hectoring, with a roll of old notes in his pocket and an exact knowledge of how much cheaper lead should be when both parties know that it's been stolen.

'I'm not buying just now, son,' he said.

Callan said, 'My name is Callan. Charlie wants to see me,' then waited. Behind the gross man a buzzer sounded.

'You see?' said Callan.

'You're to wait in the gallery,' the gross man said. 'You go first.'

That was one thing you never forgot – the obsessive caution of your trade. Always you got the other man to go first if you could; always you walked behind, out of reach of a back kick or a flailing, probing arm. But this time Callan didn't mind being first; he'd left the game, and anyway, Charlie had sent for him, and Charlie didn't like his visitors hurt till he'd had the chance to talk to them.

He walked down the corridor that reeked still of disinfectant, chalk, stale air and an elusive scent of boy, pushed open the swing-doors and entered what had been the assembly hall, but now it had been converted into a shooting gallery, a narrow steel-clad alley cut into the squareness of the room, its sides

protected by thick wads of telephone directories. On a bench in front were the weapons,
ready for practice: the Colt and Smith and
Wesson 38 revolvers, the 9-mm. Browning
semi-automatics. In front of the bench,
another man stood, one hand over the waistband of his trousers. A tall, lean man, with a
languid grace of body and a hungry mouth.

Callan grinned. 'Take it easy, Meres,' he
said. 'I haven't come here to kill anybody.'

'It's just routine, Callan,' said Meres. 'You
should remember that at least.'

The hand at his waist tightened.

'Over to the wall please. Let Vic have a
look at you.'

Callan leaned forward, palms flat on the
wall and Vic searched him: a painstaking business, with no regard at all for any embarrassment the subject might have had.

'He's clean,' said Vic.

'Splendid,' said Meres. 'Let's go and call
on Charlie.'

The corridor again, and more boy smell,
and again Callan walked ahead and an expert
followed. Callan reached the door marked
'Secretary', opened it, went inside.

She hadn't changed either. Sometimes
Callan thought that nothing could change
her. She sat at her desk and was neat and

impersonal and efficient – and beautiful. An English rose: the dew on it frozen to a diamond hardness. Hunter treated her as if she were sixty, and covered in warts. It was the only way to live with her.

'You're to go in,' she said.

Not even How are you? Not even Hallo?

The two men moved forward.

'Alone,' she said.

Callan turned, quickly. Meres was scowling.

'Mr. Meres is to wait at the target range,' she said.

Callan went through the door marked 'Headmaster'.

It was as it had always been. The battered, mahogany desk, prized possession of an Edwardian autocrat with a Bible in one hand and a cane in the other; the overstuffed swivel chair; the bank of T.V. screens that ceaselessly monitored every approach to the building, every room and corridor inside it.

'Hallo, Hunter,' said Callan.

The man at the desk hadn't changed either. The suit was old but well-pressed, the shirt gleaming clean, the tie discreet and tightly knotted, the hands, spotless as a surgeon's, comfortably relaxed. And the face too was the same. Callan had once had nightmares

12

about that face for fifteen consecutive nights, and the most frightening thing about it was that it never altered. It was an establishment face; long-nosed, thin-mouthed. The chin was square, but not unduly aggressive, the eyes a clear grey, the hair thinning now, but ruthlessly cut at Trumpers every other week, the body enviably slim, though Hunter hated exercise. A man whose predominant characteristics would be intelligence and patience. Probably a planner, somewhere in the top echelons of the Civil Service. A decision taker. Good family background, public school and all that. Oxford too. Something of a scholar. Three thousand a year and the chance of a knighthood when he retired. Hunter was all of that. He was, besides, a man who arranged executions. That was what his section was for: the elimination of undesirables. For seven years Callan had worked for him, before the nightmares started.

'You're looking well,' Hunter said. 'Sleeping better?'

'Every night.'

'Still drinking?'

'At the boozer,' said Callan. 'I don't keep the stuff at home. Can't afford to.'

'Ah, yes. The job. How is the job? Boring,

I gather.'

'How d'you gather that?' Callan asked.

'I asked,' Hunter said. 'And that employer of yours – a boor, I believe.'

'A bastard,' said Callan. 'You picked him.'

Hunter looked pained.

'After all, there isn't much demand for chaps like you once you leave me,' he said. 'I do my best of course – but your talents are so specialized. What *can* you do, after all? Use a gun, use your fists, open locks. Legally, you're unskilled, Callan.'

Callan said, 'I'd have done better robbing banks.' Hunter's look of pain vanished. 'That's a joke,' Callan said. 'I know what you'd do if I started on that caper. And anyway–'

'Go on,' said Hunter.

'I'm not a crook,' Callan said. 'And I don't want to be.'

'You're a killer,' said Hunter. He said it quite objectively. It could have been, 'You're a Methodist.'

'I nearly got a medal for it,' Callan said.

'Are you still good with a gun?' Hunter asked.

'I think so,' said Callan. 'I haven't had much chance to find out, just recently.'

'Would you like to find out now?'

The answer must be written all over me, Callan thought. As if I was a kid, and good old Uncle Charlie's waiting to take me to the circus. Why do I love the bloody things so much? And the answer was obvious: because you're good, Callan. You're the best Hunter ever had. He even told you so, the night you said you were quitting.

He followed Hunter down to the range. Meres was still there, waiting, but as Callan walked over to the range Meres' gun was in his hand.

'Don't worry, Toby,' said Callan. 'Just practising. I don't want to kill either of you.'

There was a Smith and Wesson 38 on the bench, ready loaded. That had always been his gun. He picked it up, hefted it and looked at Hunter. Hunter had never fired a shot in his life, but he knew all there was to know about the men who did. Callan lifted the revolver, sighted, fired and swore, then fired again in a crackling stream of sound. When he had finished, Hunter wound in the target.

'One outer, one inner, three bulls,' he said.

'I'm getting rusty,' said Callan.

'You'll do,' said Hunter, and watched as Callan's hands, calm and precise, broke the gun open, punched out the shells and cleaned it.

'Much more fun than wholesale groceries, eh, Callan?' he asked.

The hands stopped, then resumed their work as Callan struggled to keep the excitement from his voice.

'You want me back?' he asked.

Hunter took his time about it.

'I didn't say that,' he said at last, and enjoyed the look on Callan's face: disappointment and bewilderment nicely blended.

'You've always been a problem to us, my dear fellow. You fight quite well, you shoot extremely well – but after all, what's my section for?'

'Getting rid of people,' said Callan, and put the gun down. Hunter flicked a look at Meres, and his gun disappeared inside his coat.

'Exactly,' Hunter said. 'Getting rid of people. Bribery, blackmail, frame-ups–'

'And death,' said Callan.

'Occasionally,' said Hunter. 'When there was no other way. In the last seven years I've had fifteen people killed. You did five of them.'

Callan winced, and Hunter, noting his cue, took him by the arm and led him back down the corridor. Meres followed behind, his coat open.

'They all had to die,' Hunter said. 'You know that. If they hadn't, they would have killed a great many innocent people. That's what security is for, Callan. The protection of the innocent.'

'And you're the judge,' said Callan. 'You decide who's innocent and who's guilty?'

'Exactly,' said Hunter. 'And you were the executioner.'

Again Callan winced, and Hunter said no more until they were back in the office, then opened the cabinet and poured three drinks: whisky and water for himself, sherry for Meres, and for Callan, whisky neat: a more than generous glass. Callan took it, and sipped. Like Meres, he held the glass in his left hand. Some habits were hard to break, and still he kept his gun-hand free, even when he no longer owned a gun.

'You worried about the innocent,' said Hunter. 'I liked that. But then you began to worry about the ones you killed, as well – and I had to let you go.'

Callan sipped again. He hadn't tasted Chivas Regal since Hunter got rid of him. Its delicate fire burned, eating away at his tensions, and he put the glass down quickly.

'Maybe I've changed,' he said.

'Because of six months in a boring job

with an unpleasant employer? I doubt it, Callan. If you're soft, you're soft. Nothing can alter that.'

Somehow Callan's hand stayed away from the glass.

'So why did you send for me?' he asked.

'If you've changed, I want you back. But I have to be sure.'

'Then we're stuck, aren't we?'

'Not necessarily,' said Hunter. 'There's a job I want done. It's urgent. Very urgent. You could do it – if you had the guts.'

'You want me to kill a man,' Callan said, and willed himself to show no emotion.

'I want more,' said Hunter. 'I want you to do it on your own. No help from the section – not even a gun. I want you to do the whole thing on your own.'

Callan's glance flicked to Meres, then away.

'I suppose you have a reason,' he said. 'You always had a reason, Hunter. For everything.'

'I have to know you've changed,' said Hunter. 'I have to be sure. I fight a war. And it never stops. People like you get battle fatigue. They crack. Sometimes they come back to me and say they're all right again. As you are doing.' Callan gave no answer.

'You look all right, but I have to be sure. In

everything I do, every decision I take. And you are a very big decision. I want proof, Callan.'

Callan said, 'Like a death?'

Hunter said, 'Nothing else will convince me.'

He opened the briefcase and took out a file, handed it to Callan. Its cover was red.

'You remember my filing system?' Hunter asked.

Remember it mate? I still have nightmares about it. If a bloke joined the wrong party you gave him a blue file. If he needed surveillance it was a yellow one. If he was dangerous – really dangerous – he got a red one, and sometimes he got killed as well. A whole bloody world of primary colours – and I got all the red ones. The traitors. The hunted. The ones who killed.

'Yes,' said Callan. 'I remember. What's this one done?'

'Never mind. He's got a red file. And he won't be in London long. You'll have to be quick,' said Hunter, and opened the file. The face that looked at Callan was bluff, hearty, strong. A well-fed face, and a tough one too. A face Callan had seen before.

'Schneider?' he said.

'You know him then,' said Hunter.

'Of course I know him,' Callan said. 'He's got the office across the hall from ours–' He broke off, angry at his own stupidity. 'Now there's a coincidence for you,' he said.

'He has to die,' said Hunter, 'and you may be the man for the job.'

'What's he done?'

'That is the second time you have asked that question. It isn't your concern. Your business is execution and nothing else – not clouding your mind with reason and explanation. Do as you're told and do it without question. Or get out now. He's in a red file, Callan. That's reason enough.'

'All right,' said Callan. 'All right.'

'You have a week. No more,' said Hunter. 'Well?'

'I'd like to see the target range again first,' said Callan.

'Very well,' said Hunter. 'I'll come down with you.'

They went back to the range, and again Meres followed, but this time his gun stayed holstered as Callan emptied the Smith and Wesson into the target. He put it down at last and picked up another, a 38 centre-fire magnum revolver with a three-inch barrel.

'This one's new,' said Callan. 'I like it.'

He looked at the name engraved on the

butt: Noguchi.

'I want an answer, Callan,' said Hunter.

Callan fired, spacing the five shots steady and even, then wound in. The bull was obliterated.

'I'll do it,' said Callan.

'Now you're sure you can? Very sensible,' said Hunter. 'Of course you realize that once you leave here you're on your own?'

'I always am,' said Callan, and left.

For the first time since Callan had entered the Headquarters, Meres relaxed, his breath coming out in a long sigh.

'What do you think?' Hunter asked.

'He's still damn good with a pistol,' said Meres.

'But will he kill Schneider?'

'He's still asking questions, sir,' Meres said. 'Why not leave Schneider to me?'

'Because Callan is a better shot, and a very resourceful young man.'

Meres scowled, and Hunter cursed, deep in his mind, the fact that all his killers were prima donnas, and he the only impresario.

'Of course, dear boy, you are resourceful too. That goes without saying. And I have another job for you. I want you to have Callan watched – round the clock. See that nothing goes wrong. If Callan gets another attack of conscience, you may have to kill Schneider yourself.'

'And Callan, sir?' Meres asked.

'If you are as resourceful as I think, you might even have Callan suspected. Why not? We don't want the section involved do we, Toby?'

CHAPTER TWO

To get back to the City, Callan needed two buses and a tube. It was a tedious and irritating journey, but Callan needed every minute of it. Shrouded in humanity, smelling it, feeling its warmth, he relaxed enough to think of what had happened, what he must now do. First the interview. He'd laid off the Scotch, and his hand and eye were still good. With practice – and that was something he must arrange for – he would be back to where he had been the night Donner had died. And Hunter wanted him badly, there could be no doubt of that. He'd sent for him, tested him – even the Chivas Regal was a booby-trap – and he'd liked what he'd seen. Do this job for Hunter, and Callan would be back in. He was sure of it. But could he do the job?

Killing had been easy at first, in Malaya. It was easy because it was the only choice offered: kill or be killed, and that way it's always easy, for the survivors. And the longer you survive, the easier it gets. Callan had been a Commando corporal then, and nearby had been a battalion of Gurkhas. He had listened to his instructors, and watched the little brown men, and he'd *learned*. He'd discovered too that he was a natural shot. He didn't miss: on good days he couldn't miss, and the men in his half-section were glad to have him with them. He was a natural. Like the rest of them, he hated the jungle, but he alone used it as the Chinese had done, making it work against the enemy, forcing them out into the open to where his half-section waited, and the rifle in Callan's hands cracked, and for once Chairman Mao's thoughts on guerrilla warfare had been no good at all...

In the jungle there were no problems. And at first when he worked for the section it hadn't been so hard. They'd picked him up after he came out of the Scrubs, and a prison is a good place to learn about survival. They'd tested him and trained him, and he'd killed Naismith for them. Naismith was a bastard who'd deserved to die, and Callan had done it with the calm certainty of his marksmanship, as if Naismith had been a tiger escaped from a zoo. And then there had been the others, the ones who'd fought back. Bunin had put a bullet through his shoulder:

it still ached on cold, damp days. Orthez had been almost too quick for him, Megali had tried to ambush. But Donner had been a good man, according to his lights, and Donner had wept...

He got off the tube at the Bank and walked slowly to his office. He was late, he knew, but he needed time to think. Schneider had to die, and maybe Callan was the one to kill him, but if he did he would have to have a reason, whatever Hunter said. If the reason were the right one he'd do it: if not he'd go on keeping Waterman's books, a vegetable working for a rat. He reached the grimy block of offices and trudged up the stairs, remembering Hunter's standard advice to his executioners: Be sure, and keep it simple. That's all there was to it – if the victim knew his part as well. Simple target, he thought, simple pistol, simple killer. Bang bang. Then Schneider walked right into him, the burly body slamming him back against the wall, as Callan's hands groped for balance and knocked a box from his hands. The lid flew open, and a dozen soldiers of the Young Guard lay on their backs among green velvet, their muskets aimed at his heart.

The impressions raced and jumbled in Callan's mind. How well dressed Schneider was, and how shabby he himself looked, his raincoat worn, his shoes mended yet again instead of thrown away. Then there were the soldiers, a dozen of them, hand-painted at a guinea a-piece, and his confused memories of their originals, their column shattered at Waterloo by Wellington's line, knowing for the first time the meaning of failure: La Garde recule. And then there was Schneider, who looked as if he had never known failure in his life, crouched over his model soldiers, checking that they weren't broken. Callan admired the competence of his hard, deft hands, and bent down, uselessly, to help.

Pushing fifty, he thought. But hard with it. Good muscles. Good nerves. He won't panic easy, not this one. He looked again at the elegant suit of lightweight tweed. The lapels on the left side were lower than those on the right. Carries a gun sometimes, he thought. Draws right-handed. And he carried a red file all the time – and doesn't know a damn thing about it.

Schneider opened the box again, showing the other soldiers inside it, checking carefully, and Callan looked at them enviously.

'Aren't they the Rifle Brigade?' he asked. 'Wellington's men?'

'They are indeed,' Schneider said, and

picked up another, a cavalryman. 'Do you know this one, by any chance?'

'That's the enemy,' said Callan. 'A Polish lancer.'

'And this?'

Schneider picked up another exquisitely modelled figure, an infantryman this time.

'An ally,' said Callan. 'The King's German Legion.'

'My favourite,' said Schneider. 'Mr...?'

'Callan.'

'So,' said Schneider, and bowed. It was a stiff and yet friendly bow, that reflected exactly the quality of his English.

'They are my favourites because I used to be a German,' he said. 'We fought very well for Wellington.'

'Right from the Torres Vedras,' said Callan. 'They were all over Spain too, weren't they? Talavera, Badajoz, Fuentes d'Onoro–'

'I think I see another madman,' said Schneider. 'Do you also collect model soldiers?'

'Yes,' Callan said. 'I fight old battles with them.'

'So do I,' said Schneider. 'It was a habit I picked up at military college. And you?'

Callan smiled. 'Military college? I was a corporal. Twice. I just like playing soldiers.'

'*Twice* a corporal?' Schneider asked. The idea seemed an impossibility to him, like a squared circle.

'I didn't get on with officers,' said Callan.

Schneider looked at him. His eyes were blue, and very clear.

'I was an officer,' he said.

Callan sensed the first intimation of combat between them, but there was something else, too: something that could develop into respect, even affection.

'You weren't on our side, Mr. Schneider,' he said.

Schneider laughed with the unconcern of a man whose teeth are perfect.

'So you know my name?' he said. 'It is good to be a man that people remember. You work for Waterman, don't you?'

Callan nodded.

'Have you a moment?' Schneider asked. 'I want to show you something.'

Callan remembered how late he was, but already Schneider had turned away, not waiting for an answer, and gone back down the corridor to a door marked: R. Schneider. Imports and Exports. He opened the door with a key on a silver chain. A Parkinson key, thought Callan. You know your locks, Mr. Schneider.

The two men entered a large room that was the untidiest Callan had ever seen. There was a desk overflowing with papers, files, invoices, orders scattered on the floor, a vase full of dead flowers, an umbrella on the window-sill – and on a table in one corner, a haven of tidiness: a neat array of soldiers, marching in two columns of fours, and in the middle artillery, horses, limbers and guns. Callan went to it at once, and again Schneider laughed, like a schoolmaster with an apt and eager pupil.

'Come,' he said. 'What do you make of this?'

'It's the Rifle Brigade again,' said Callan, and picked up one of the perfectly proportioned pieces as memory stirred. 'Black Bob Crauford's men?'

'Excellent,' said Schneider. 'Perfect. And in the middle?'

'The Chestnut troop of the Royal Horse Artillery,' said Callan. 'They marched all day to join Wellington at Talavera.' He picked up the gun-carriage, examined it, put it back precisely where it was.

'It's beautiful,' he said.

'Such a word for an Englishman to use,' said Schneider, but his mockery was gentle.

'They marched forty miles in twenty hours

with full pack and equipment. In Spain. At the height of summer. One hundred and sixty years ago – when the men were like gods.'

The clear blue eyes held Callan's again, innocent and happy, but behind him Callan could see the wires of a burglar-alarm system on the window-ledge, and a very good system it was.

'Did you like being in the army?' Schneider asked.

'Sometimes,' said Callan.

'I also,' said Schneider. 'Sometimes. But playing soldiers is better. All the time. Here it is all brilliance and triumph and splendour – no blood. I do not care for blood, Mr. Callan. Not any more.'

'Me neither,' said Callan. But that wasn't the truth, or not the whole truth anyway. He looked at his watch and found he had to leave. That was good. He could not stay longer with this man whom he liked so much.

'I'm sorry, Mr. Schneider,' he said. 'I have to get back to work.'

'Of course,' said Schneider, and his voice was grave. 'I'm a capitalist myself. It is right that you should be exploited.' Then the smile came. 'But come and see my soldiers again. Whenever you like.'

'Thanks,' said Callan, and left, walking down the dreary corridor that always smelled, inexplicably, of boot-polish, and far too explicably of cat. The outer door of Waterman's office hadn't been painted for years, its frosted glass was stained, and the words 'J. G. Waterman, Wholesale Grocer', painted on the glass, had lost so much paint that they no longer had meaning. Deliberately Callan kicked the door before he opened it. There'd be a row anyway, and he wanted to get it over. To Callan, rows with Waterman were the ultimate boredom; to Waterman they were the breath of life. Callan thought: We might as well be married and have done with it, then opened the door.

Waterman was fleshy, seedy and not nearly rich enough to be happy. His lunch consisted invariably of two large gins, a pork pie and pickles, and always after lunch he was dyspeptic. He was dyspeptic now, and eager for battle.

'And what time is this, may I ask?' he said.

Callan looked at his watch.

'Two fifteen,' he said.

Waterman looked at his watch, and said, 'No, it's not. It's seventeen minutes past.'

'Thanks,' said Callan, and moved his

watch on two minutes. Waterman took a step forward.

'And what time does your lunch-hour terminate?' he yelled.

'Two o'clock,' said Callan. 'I'm a bit late.'

'No,' said Waterman. 'No. Not a bit late. You are seventeen minutes late. There are only the two of us, Callan, and my place is there' – He pointed a meaty finger at the door to his own office – 'not waiting out here for my assistant to honour me with his presence.'

Callan gave up, as he always did.

'Yes, Mr. Waterman,' he said.

'And what precisely does that mean?'

Callan studied the places where he could hit Waterman and kill him, or better still, cripple him for life, then thrust his hands deep in his pockets and clenched his fists.

'It means you do belong in there, Mr. Waterman, and I belong out here, because I'm a peasant.'

'You are, you are indeed,' said Waterman, 'and a tardy one at that. I'd like the Owen invoices completed by this evening.'

Callan went to his desk, picked up the invoices and banged them down.

'You can have them now,' he said.

Waterman picked them up and examined

them slowly and with care. His face saddened: there were no mistakes.

'You can be industrious, when you *do* come to work,' he said at last.

Compliments, thought Callan. This won't do.

'That's the peasant in me,' he said. 'I know nothing but toil. I thrive on curses. Kindness is beyond my understanding.'

'Then it's just as well you're in my employ,' said Waterman. 'I want the Johnson Stores Account for tomorrow morning.'

Callan tugged at his forelock as Waterman slammed his door. Seventeen minutes, he thought. What about all the overtime he gets out of me for nothing? He took off his coat and prepared to do battle with Johnson's Stores. Waterman's book-keeping was as hazy as his honesty, but there was a great deal of satisfaction in tackling a messy jumble like this and arranging its chaos into the order tax inspectors insist on. Gradually the figures fell into a pattern, and as he worked, a part of Callan's mind nagged at the problem that waited. Schneider had seemed all right. At least he treated you like a man... It should be Waterman inside the red file. Waterman was a rat. Mean, greedy, vicious. Schneider now – Schneider was big and easygoing – confident.

He could afford to be – tough and shrewd as he was. And happy, Callan thought. I liked his laughter. But he carries a gun sometimes, I'm sure – and he's got a hell of a good burglar alarm. That lock on his door won't blow open either. Then the figures claimed him, and he worked on till another idea clamoured for an answer.

I wonder what the hell he's done? thought Callan. But there was no future in that one, and he dismissed it, sticking to his arithmetic until the thing was almost finished and he could relax and brew tea. He picked up the kettle and was on his way to the washroom when he heard footsteps in the corridor. The visitors could only be for Waterman, or Schneider. He pulled in the washroom door and watched, and listened.

There were two men, tall, well built, wearing raincoats over their suits, and trilby hats. They didn't hurry, and their walk was purposeful. Fraud Squad? Callan wondered. Have they caught up with Waterman at last? But it was Schneider's door they stopped at, and one of them knocked with that 'I know you're in there' knock. Schneider answered, taking his time, but bluff and genial still.

'Yes?' he said.

The older man said, 'Mr. Schneider? Mr.

Rudolf Schneider?'

'Yes?' said Schneider again.

The older one said, 'I'm Detective Inspector Pollard. This is Detective Sergeant Grace. We'd like to talk to you, please.'

'By all means,' said Schneider, and leaned against the lintel of the door.

Pollard sighed. The scene was a familiar one, but he still detested it.

'May we come in, sir?' he asked. 'It's – rather confidential.'

'Secrets?' said Schneider. 'You want to tell me secrets? Come in, gentlemen. Come in at once.'

He stood aside and they entered, then he shut the door. Callan left the washroom and stood outside Schneider's office. The voices were faint, only just audible, but at least he could listen now, and learn, and perhaps make up his mind.

CHAPTER THREE

Pollard and Grace went at once to the table that held the model soldiers, and for one brief instant they looked like boys in a toy-shop at Christmas. Behind them, Schneider chuckled.

'A hobby,' he said. 'To you it must seem very childish, but hobbies have that effect on grown men.' He paused, and the two police-men waited stolidly. 'Sit down please, gentle-men.' They sat down and took off their hats, and Schneider waited. His self-possession was absolute.

At last Pollard said, 'Well, sir, we realize you're a very busy man–'

'Of course,' said Schneider. 'I make a great deal of money. What do you want to tell me?'

'Nothing, sir,' said Pollard, and Schneider grinned his appreciation at a point scored. 'It's more like ask you, really.'

'You wish to know *my* secrets? Remember I'm a business man, Inspector.'

And there it was. The first real move.

'What exactly is your business, Mr. Schneider?' Pollard asked.

Schneider said at once, 'I import and export.'

'What?' asked Pollard.

'Anything. Anything at all – that I can buy cheap and sell dear.'

Pollard made no perceptible movement, but it was Grace's turn.

'Where from, sir?' the detective sergeant asked.

'Which? The buying or the selling?'

'Both sir – if you don't mind telling us,' said Grace.

'Mind?' said Schneider. 'Why should I mind? My God, how polite you are.'

He pulled open two drawers and dumped great heaps of invoices on the desk top, then picked up handfuls at random.

'See for yourself,' he said. 'Chile, Switzerland, Canada, Morocco, South Africa, Portugal, Monaco. Anywhere at all my dear chap.' He showered the invoice slips on the two policemen, they looked at his desk in dismay.

'Excuse me,' he said. 'I am a very untidy fellow.'

Grace took Pollard's invoice slips and his own, and coaxed them into a neat pile.

'Did you ever export to the Indonesian Republic, sir?' he asked.

'I think not,' said Schneider, 'but it will take me some time to check. Oh, my dear chap – if only I had a system.'

Pollard asked, 'Did you ever import from Japan?'

'Oh, yes,' said Schneider. 'All the time. One does you know. It may not be very sporting, but it's extremely cheap.'

'What did you import, sir?' asked Grace.

Schneider said at once, 'Motor-bicycles, transistor radios, cameras. And novelties.'

'Novelties?' asked Grace.

'What a persistent young man you are,' said Schneider. He went to a cupboard, pulled out a flat rubber cushion and laid it on his desk. 'Press on that please,' he said. Grace hesitated. 'As a favour to me,' said Schneider.

Grace did as he asked and the cushion deflated with a prolonged and very vulgar raspberry.

'You see?' said Schneider. 'Novelties.' Then his face expanded in a beam of comprehension, and Pollard and Grace winced for what was to come.

'Ah, now I understand,' he said. 'You think I sell pornographic novelties. No no, gentlemen. It is all simple vulgarity – for the Christmas trade.'

Grace folded the cushion and handed it back to Schneider, who at once reinflated it.

Outside the door, Callan smiled. Schneider was handling this one like a grand master playing mere experts. It was a joy to hear. And then suddenly he heard footsteps and only just got back to his room in time. It was Bethany, the rep for Nature Foods. Nature Foods were terrible, and Bethany was worse. Waterman's orders were that he must never, never see him. Callan prepared to waste five minutes keeping Bethany from the presence. What he'd heard so far had been valuable, but what he was missing was the real meat. It was hard to feel sorry for Bethany – this time.

Pollard said, 'Have you dealt with a firm called Noguchi of Yokohama?'

Schneider pawed vaguely at the precarious pile of invoices.

'What do they sell, Sergeant?' he asked.

'Guns,' said Pollard.

'Cowboy six-shooters? Atomic ray-guns? Water-pistols?'

Grace said, 'No, sir. Real guns. Rifles, machine-guns. Revolvers.'

'But how could I, Sergeant?' said

Schneider. 'Where could I take them to?'

'Hong Kong, sir,' said Pollard. 'Under bond.'

Grace said, 'The Hong Kong police think you do, sir.'

'You have come to arrest me?' Schneider asked.

'No, sir, we couldn't for that. But where you send them to afterwards–' said Grace.

'This is just a little chat,' said Pollard. 'Nothing official.'

'Is that why you bring a witness?' Schneider asked, his smile more jovial than ever.

'Time you stopped it,' said Pollard. 'You're too well known.'

Then Grace's line: 'They'll get you next time, Mr. Schneider.'

And Pollard pronounced the Amen. 'They'll put you down for ten years. You just remember that.'

They got up to leave then, and Schneider watched them go. As they passed through the door he pressed with both fists on the whoopee cushion. Neither man reacted. Schneider got up from the desk and walked to the table, then picked up the gun-carriage. He did nothing with it: only looked at it. His hands were quite steady.

Callan watched Pollard and Grace leave,

then tried to persuade Bethany to do the same.

'It's more than my job's worth, Mr. Bethany,' he said. 'You know that.'

'We've got some new lines,' said Bethany.

'We're overstocked as it is,' said Callan.

'Our prices are very keen,' Bethany said. 'Really competitive.'

Callan looked at him: a shy man in an extrovert's trade, failure the very air he breathed, and yet he stuck at it, month after month. Accepting it, thinking it was normal even. The clothes all wrong, the approach all wrong – and that terrible product.

Suddenly Bethany said, 'You're never going to let me in, are you, Mr. Callan?'

Callan said, 'I can't,' and it was true enough.

'Sometimes I think I ought to pack it in,' said Bethany. 'Lugging this case around, asking to see people – where does it get you?'

'It's a living I suppose,' said Callan.

Bethany went on unheeding: 'And even when I do get to see people, why should they buy from me? You know what this stuff is?' He kicked the case at his feet. 'Muck, that's what it is, Mr. Callan. You know – even when they do buy – I feel ashamed.'

41

Callan said, 'Maybe you ought to pack it in.'

'I'd like to,' said Bethany. 'God knows I'd like to. The trouble is you see – I've had no training. For anything.'

Tears came into the corners of his eyes, and he brushed them away. It had all happened before.

'I don't think I'd better waste any more of your time,' he said.

'I *have* got a lot to do,' said Callan, and watched as the little man staggered out with the over-large suitcase.

'You will tell him I called,' said Bethany.

'I'll tell him.'

'If he should change his mind, he knows where to reach me,' Bethany said, and struggled away.

Callan sighed, then went back to the washroom, retrieved the kettle and began to brew tea. Bethany thought his world was coming to an end because he wasn't trained, and he, Callan, had fled from his world because he'd trained too much. He waited for the kettle to boil, and brewed up. He was on his second cup when Waterman came out of the office.

'Well well,' he said. 'Refreshments. I notice I wasn't invited to partake.'

'Bethany was here,' said Callan, and Waterman scowled: this was unanswerable.

'I'm going round to see Mr. Owen,' he said. 'I may not be back.'

'I'll try not to let it get me down,' said Callan.

'I want that account on my desk before you leave.'

Callan snapped to attention: his right arm shot up in salute.

'Jawohl, Herr Obergruppenführer,' he said.

But it was no good. Waterman saluted him back, as if he really were an Obergruppenführer, and Callan the newest clumsiest recruit to the SS, and left. Waterman always won. It was inevitable. He had the money. His own tongue was sharper, Callan knew, but Waterman enjoyed the fights anyway, and even if he lost he simply walked out and left Callan to do the work for both of them. And Callan had to take it. Waterman paid bloody little, but he was the only one Hunter said he could work for. So how could he lose?

Callan went to work and finished the account, adding the finishing touches in red without thinking, until he found himself staring at the thin, scarlet lines. He started to shake then, and his hands were sweating. It was time to talk to Hunter.

He locked the outer office door, then went into Waterman's office where the phone was, and sat in Waterman's chair that was infinitely more comfortable than his own. Then he picked up the phone and dialled the special number. And when she answers, he thought, it'll be just like old times.

'Yes?' she said.

'Let me speak to Charlie, please,' said Callan.

'Who's speaking?'

Callan sighed. The drill. Always the drill, with her. The only thing she had a passion for.

'This is Callan,' he said. 'Tell Charlie it's urgent. About a friend of mine. The one in red.'

'He's busy, Mr. Callan,' she said. 'Does he have your number?'

'Yes,' Callan said.

'He'll call you back.'

Callan sat in Waterman's chair and fretted, and looked at his watch five times before the phone rang, then scooped it up at once.

'Waterman's Limited,' he said.

'Goodness,' said Hunter. 'You do sound professional. What's wrong?'

'You are,' said Callan. 'You can stuff your job.'

'How crude you are,' said Hunter, his voice a sigh. 'What's happened?'

'Your German friend. The bogeys are after him,' Callan said.

Hunter, slumped in his chair, looked across at Meres, who was listening to the conversation on an earpiece. Meres shook his head.

'Really?' said Hunter.

'Yes, really,' said Callan. 'And if they're having him watched I haven't a hope in hell. Or is that what you had in mind?'

'No indeed,' said Hunter. 'I had no idea there were such complications.'

'Well there are. So you can forget it,' Callan said.

'Wait,' said Hunter, and Callan enjoyed the rare urgency in his voice. 'If you do this job – there is a chance that I may want you back.' There was no answer. 'Are you there, Callan?'

'I'm here,' said Callan. 'I won't do it.'

'Callan, for heaven's sake – you've handled the police before,' said Hunter.

'Not when it's a rush job,' Callan said.

'All right,' said Hunter. 'I'll find out what's happening. But stay with this one. It's very,

45

very urgent.'

'Just get rid of the rozzers,' said Callan, and hung up.

Very carefully Hunter replaced his receiver. Even now, Meres noted, he showed no sign of anger, or even irritation.

'How pleased Callan must be,' Hunter said. 'He's forced me into a bargain.'

'Will you keep it, sir?' asked Meres.

'I may have to,' said Hunter, and the chair swivelled, his eyes held Meres'. 'Dear boy,' he said. 'Police. Meddling in our affairs. What on earth is happening?'

'I've no idea, sir,' Meres said.

'But you should know,' said Hunter. 'You are *paid* to know.'

'It wasn't the Special Branch, sir,' he said. 'I'm sure of that.'

'I might have to ring up the Home Office,' said Hunter. 'I should have to ask them a favour. They detest it you know.' Very briefly he smiled. 'That is some compensation.'

Meres said, 'I take it you still want me to keep a watch on Callan?'

'Certainly I do. He fascinates me. Don't you find him fascinating?'

'No, sir,' said Meres.

'He's so detestable,' Hunter said dreamily, 'and so useful. I grant you we're all like that

46

– but Callan is a worrier too. Do you ever worry, Meres?'

'Only when there's danger, sir.'

'Callan worries all the time,' said Hunter. 'Maybe that's why he's so good.'

Meres scowled, but this time Hunter did not reproach himself. Some time or other the dear boy had to learn.

Callan sat at Waterman's desk, and thought about getting a gun. There was only one way, and it would cost a lot of money – but Hunter had a lot of money, so that was no problem. But once he'd got the thing, he'd have to practise. The kind he'd need was something that could he stowed away where it wouldn't show, and that meant a 38 at the most, a Smith and Wesson Chief's Special maybe, or an Airweight. They'd got them down to fourteen ounces. But with a gun like that you had to be accurate – bloody accurate. He'd seen a man absorb three rounds from a 38 lightweight and still keep on coming. You had to hit them in the heart, or the head, probably from a snap shot, and you couldn't do that with a strange gun, so practice it had to be – once he'd got it, and to do that he had to talk to Lonely. There was nobody else he knew.

It wouldn't be easy. Lonely was as nervous as a cat at Cruft's. In the Scrubs he'd been afraid all the time: of the other cons, the screws, the hard boys who would be waiting for him when he got out. He'd been a trusty, Callan remembered, and he, Callan, had not. He'd done his bird for a first offence, but it had been a big one. Twenty-five thousand quid, he remembered, and he'd done it solo. In the Scrubs they respected you for a job like that, even when it didn't come off. Lonely had been done for housebreaking – money and goods value fifty pounds, with seventeen similar offences taken into consideration, so by the Scrubs' evaluation of things, Callan was five hundred times the man Lonely was.

It had been a nice, easy tickle. Before he went into the army, Callan had been apprenticed to Bartram's, and Bartram's made safes for half the world. He'd been a good apprentice: he'd even won their award for the best apprentice of the year: the year before he joined the army, and found out he was even better with a gun than he was with locks. And he'd done well in the army, so long as he was fighting. They made him a corporal, and there'd even been talk of a commission until he'd got drunk in Kuala

Lumpur, and then he went back to being a private, and back to the jungle, where he'd killed more terrorists for them, and got his stripes back. Then he'd saved the life of his company commander.

It was impossible, even now, to remember the madness that had taken possession of him. Captain Henshaw had been wounded, and there were six of them round him. Six small figures in jungle green with rifles and stens in their hands. Henshaw was wounded, and they were kicking him and screaming. He could remember that. But afterwards – they'd had to tell him about what happened afterwards. He'd run straight at them, all six, and shot three of them out of hand, then charged right into the others. They'd shot at him and missed, and he'd swung his rifle like a club, killed another and laid out a fifth. The sixth had made a break for it, and he'd gone after him, and when his half-section came up and found him, number six was dead too, and Callan's fingers were round his neck... He'd come out of it then, and got on the W/T and whistled up the rest of the company and some armour. But he'd caught no more terrorists... Later he found out that one of those he'd killed was a woman. He'd been twenty years old.

Henshaw had been loud in praise. That made the whole thing even more inexplicable. He detested Henshaw, and had thought it was mutual, but the man went on and on about it. There was talk of a medal: a DCM at least, and Callan had gone on a drunken binge with a couple of friends who were as puzzled as he was. They admired him for it, but they didn't like it. The Callan they liked shot from cover and killed: he didn't risk their lives by chancing his own against Chinese marksmanship. So they'd got drunk with him to cover up their dislike, and there'd been a fight and Callan had half-killed a REME sergeant. They took his tapes away again, and there was no medal, but at least he missed military prison. Henshaw went back to detesting him, and Callan never again went mad...

When he was demobbed he went back to Bartram's, but he'd lost too much time, and there was no excitement in making safes. And Callan needed excitement; it was a part of life. So he'd helped put in a new safe in a supermarket, and walked in cool as you please one Saturday night, opened it up and started to help himself. And even that hadn't been exciting. Not that part of it. He didn't really want the money, and the risk of getting in, of opening up the safe, had been no risk at all. Not like Malaya. Excitement didn't happen till the watchman found him, and he could have taken the watchman with no trouble at all. Any one of the half dozen blows he'd used on that REME sergeant would have finished him easy. But it might have finished him for good, and Callan couldn't risk it. So the old boy grabbed him and yelled bloody murder, and a policeman had been passing, and Callan had got two years.

The judge had a lot to say about abusing a position of trust, Callan remembered. That meant that people who trained at Bartram's then robbed safes were even bigger bastards than the other bastards who robbed safes. He'd also told him he was lucky he hadn't croaked the old watchman, since he'd had Commando training. The way Callan looked at it, it was the watchman who was lucky. His luck was in getting just two years – and maybe in meeting Lonely.

They'd been three in a cell for a bit. It was always one or three: two might turn out to be immoral. The third had been some kind of religious maniac who'd tried to burn down a Congregational chapel and prayed all the time. He needed nobody. God was with him, waking and sleeping, he told them, and with nobody else. But Lonely needed Callan, needed particularly his ability to endure prison life without fear. At twenty-three, there wasn't much Callan was afraid of. His body was hard, his mind detached and his Commando skill beyond anything the hard boys in his block could muster. He had three fights in his two years. The first two he won easily. The third was against three men. He won that too, but it put him in the hospital with the other three, and for some reason it cost him his remission. Prison was like that.

It had been about tobacco, Callan remembered. The three men had been trying to form a snout syndicate, and they knew Callan didn't smoke. They wanted him to sell his allowance to them, but he'd refused. Lonely was already getting him a good price from the tobacco baron in his block. After that they'd tried to work him over, and Callan – and they – had taken a beating. The last one had broken his arm. When it healed, he came out, saw the governor, lost his remission, and waited. Smedley, the first of the three, had left hospital for the punishment cells. He did seven days on bread and water, returned to the block, and Callan put him back in the hospital. There were no witnesses

– there never are – and Callan waited for the other two. But instead, he'd been put in a cell of his own one night, and a bunch of warders came in and beat him, scientifically, where it wouldn't show. And Callan had enough detachment left to take it. Thy didn't hurt him too much, and anyway it was their nick. They couldn't go on having fights all the time... The other two men did their punishment and were transferred to Parkhurst.

It was Lonely who had helped him after the warders' beating – the way the mouse helped the lion, Callan thought – and maybe the mouse expected a kick-back all the time. But when Callan was a mass of bruises it was Lonely who bathed them – the religious maniac prayed right through the whole episode – and Lonely who passed the word to the snout baron so that Callan was never bothered again. Lonely had done his best, Callan thought, but Jesus he smelled. Screws were always sending him to the baths. But it wasn't that. Lonely always smelled when he was frightened, and he was frightened all the time – until Callan recovered. Then he was under Callan's protection, and the fear died, until Callan got out. After that he smelled again, worrying about some geezer called Rinty who was going to carve him when he got out. Callan had gone to see Rinty and found his Scrubs reputation had preceded him. Never never, Rinty swore, would he harm a friend of Mr. Callan's. And Callan had told Lonely so, the day before a man from Hunter's section had offered him a job... Lonely wasn't in a position to deny Callan a favour. Besides, he'd seen Callan in action, and he feared Callan most of all. And Lonely could get you things – even guns. British crooks were not supposed to be what the admen called gun orientated, but they did use them now and again: on security guards, on policemen, even on each other, and people like Lonely could be made to act as suppliers. The little man had the most comprehensive system of underworld connections Callan had ever heard of, mostly through his family, which was enormous, and bent to a man – and woman. All he had to do now was find Lonely. And that meant pubs.

CHAPTER FOUR

It took him a while to realize he was being followed. The men Meres had put on him were good. There were three of them, and a car, but the car was useless. Callan set off walking and two of the others followed. The third man rang up headquarters on the R/T and was told to come in. Two men, Meres thought, would be enough...

Callan walked to the tube and the rain started again. He turned up his collar and walked on. Behind him was a man in a brown overcoat and behind him a City type in an Aquascutum raincoat and a rolled umbrella so exquisite that he kept it rolled, even when the rain fell harder. Callan waited at a red light and noticed the umbrella. He walked on, and Rolled Umbrella lagged, but Brown overcoat stayed right behind him. They still held their positions when they got to the tube-station. Callan asked for Piccadilly, and the man behind took a ticket to Green Park. Rolled Umbrella had a pass, but he wasted time buying an *Evening Standard* so that

Callan was again ahead of him when he went down the escalator, but now Brown Overcoat was leading as they boarded the tube that would take them to Holborn.

There they changed to the Piccadilly Line, and Callan and Brown Overcoat shared a non-smoker. Rolled Umbrella took a smoker further back and produced a cigar just to make it look authentic. By this time, Callan was sure that they were following him, and his mind sought for reasons. It couldn't be Schneider: there was no possible way in which Schneider could know about him – so that left only Hunter. But why? There could only be one reason: to see that he was doing his job properly. And that was fair enough, in a way. But Callan liked to work alone: secrecy was a part of his system: even of his life. He didn't want Hunter to know how he did things: only that they had been done.

The train pulled into Leicester Square. Callan took a newspaper out of his pocket, yawned and began to read. At the last possible moment he darted out between the closing doors, and Brown Overcoat had lost a customer – but Rolled Umbrella was there, waiting on the platform as he'd waited on every platform since Callan boarded the train. Not bad, Callan conceded. Not bad at all. After all, every tube train has its eccentric. He went to the escalator and Rolled Umbrella followed, the umbrella tapping as he walked.

Brown Overcoat got off at the next stop and rang in. To his surprise, Hunter was delighted.

'I hoped he'd spot you,' he said. 'Was he good?'

'The best,' said Brown Overcoat, and meant it. To get away from him Callan had to be that, and he had been, in that single instant when his body exploded from utter relaxation to that carefully calculated leap.

'I didn't even know he was on to me,' he said. 'But Jones is still with him.'

'Good,' said Hunter. 'Good.' His hand was flicking through Callan's file. It had a yellow cover. 'He took a ticket to Piccadilly?'

'Yes, sir,' Brown Overcoat said.

Hunter found the place in the file he was looking for. 'He may have gone to meet a friend of his,' he said. 'A rather smelly friend.' He began to describe Lonely. 'He uses one of four or five pubs in Piccadilly,' said Hunter, and listed them. 'Go and find him, will you – and see if Callan joins him. And go at once. Take a taxi. Spare no expense.' He hung up and looked at the picture of Callan in the front of his file. It had been taken four years ago, and already there was doubt in the eyes, but there was no mistaking the driving force of will there too.

Hunter thought, It's possible I should feel sorry for Jones. I hope so.

Callan took him for a walk. It took time to find the kind of spot he needed. It had to be quiet, and it had to have a succession of sharp corners. The one he chose at last was just what he needed. Rolled Umbrella was wary of the first corner, and the second. Callan strolled on unheeding, then speeded up at the third corner. By the time Rolled Umbrella reached the fourth, he was moving like a light infantryman. Callan waited behind it, and struck as Rolled Umbrella came hurtling round. The blow came from the edge of his hand, and struck at the nerve just below Rolled Umbrella's nose. Rolled Umbrella rocked on his feet, and his bones seemed to turn liquescent so that he sagged inside his skin. Callan caught him and propped him against the wall. He slid down it slowly, like a drunk in a silent comedy.

'You're a disgrace to the regiment, sir,' said Callan, and bent the umbrella across his knee.

He found Lonely at last in 'The Peal of Bells', a big, anonymous pub that welcomed everybody from Wardour Street film executives to barrow boys from the Berwick market. Lonely was at the bar, drinking a pint of bitter, and Callan reached out a hand in the time-honoured gesture and grasped Lonely's shoulder. Lonely jumped, and spilled beer down his shirt-front, then turned, warily. Callan looked at him, not smiling, and Lonely found the nerve to be indignant.

'I don't think that's very funny, Mr. Callan,' he said.

'I do,' said Callan, then froze. Three places away, a man was nursing a lager as if it had to last a long, long time. It was Brown Overcoat. Lonely continued to mop at his shirt-front.

'I'll buy you a drink,' said Callan. 'What do you want?'

'Scotch and water,' said Lonely.

Callan pushed up to the bar. Brown Overcoat didn't look at him. He bought a large Scotch and water and a pint of bitter, and led Lonely to a table. Somebody fed money into a jukebox and the noise, loud before, became only just bearable. It was a very useful pub. Callan handed Lonely the beer and said 'Cheers.'

'Scotch gives me heartburn anyway,' said Lonely, and sucked at his pint. Callan sat, waiting, as the little man observed his shabby raincoat, the grease-mark on his suit, the shirt that should have been at the laundry. Then Callan's eyes, pale and un-winking, held Lonely's.

'I'm in disguise,' Callan said at last.

'I knew you wouldn't dress like that, Mr. Callan,' Lonely said. 'Been away?'

'I'm never going back inside,' said Callan. 'I've been resting. Now I'm back at work.'

At once there came the smell.

'God,' said Callan. 'No wonder they call you Lonely. Don't you ever take a bath?'

Lonely said, 'We been through all that before, Mr. Callan.'

Brown Overcoat got up and went to the 'Gents'. Callan sat in silence till the door closed.

'You can help me,' he said then.

'I'm sorry, Mr. Callan,' Lonely said. 'Of course I'd like to help you, but I'm not at liberty myself. I got a lot of odd jobs piling up–'

This wouldn't do at all.

'You stink,' said Callan. 'D'you know that?' Lonely sat in huddled misery. 'You're a one man sewage farm.'

Lonely tried to rise then.

'I don't like insults, Mr. Callan,' he said. Callan's arm reached out, holding Lonely to his chair as Brown Overcoat went back to the bar.

'Drink your nice beer,' Callan said, 'and don't get me mad.'

Lonely drank, his hand shaking.

'I don't want an assistant,' said Callan. 'I want a gun.'

Lonely's hand shook more than ever.

'Guns is bad, Mr. Callan,' said Lonely. 'They can get you ten years.'

'I'm worse,' said Callan. 'And you know it.'

Lonely sighed.

'I want a Smith and Wesson 38 Airweight revolver and a box of shells. How much will it cost me?'

'A hundred quid,' said Lonely.

'All right,' said Callan. 'COD.'

'Mr. Callan, I haven't got that kind of money,' Lonely said.

'Open your piggy-bank,' said Callan. 'And get it for me quick.'

'There's a geezer I know been over to Paris,' said Lonely. 'He might have one.'

'Tell him it's for you,' said Callan.

Lonely looked more miserable than ever.

'Do you think he'd believe me?' he asked.

Brown Overcoat pushed his way towards a telephone kiosk.

'No. Guns are for experts,' Callan said. They have to be. They go off.'

'You used one before, Mr. Callan?' Lonely asked.

'Yes,' said Callan. 'I've used one.' He watched Lonely's hand shake. 'Put your beer down,' he said. 'You're wasting it.'

Brown Overcoat waited outside the phone booth and Callan reached out for an empty cigarette packet and folded it into a wedge. Lonely put down his beer.

'Bring the thing to my place,' said Callan. 'Flat 3, Stanmore House, Duke William Street, Bayswater. Got it?' Lonely repeated it back to him.

'Good man,' said Callan, and clapped him on the shoulder.

Lonely winced. 'Just remember it, Lonely. Don't write it down.'

Lonely said bitterly, 'You know I can't write, Mr. Callan.'

Brown Overcoat went into the phone booth and Callan rose.

'Come and see me tomorrow,' said Callan. 'Seven o'clock. And buy some soap before you come. I'll pay for it.'

He pushed his way through the crowd at the bar, then paused by the telephone box and bent as if to tie his shoe. As he did so, he pushed the folded cigarette packet like a wedge in the bottom of the door. When he straightened up, he found that Brown Overcoat was looking straight at him. Callan winked, and walked out briskly as Brown Overcoat beat on the door like a man with claustrophobia. Soho swallowed Callan whole, and he pushed on to Shaftesbury Avenue and a taxi. The whole exercise had been ridiculous, he knew. Hunter knew where he lived, and there'd be another man waiting for him there. But at least he'd demonstrated to Hunter that he was dangerous still – and on top of his job. He'd be even more dangerous the following night at seven. Then he'd have a gun.

When Brown Overcoat persuaded a barman to release him he went back to the section at once. Mr. Meres' instructions had been quite explicit, and Mr. Meres was not a man to cross, particularly if anything went wrong. Meres, Brown Overcoat knew, was a killer – you couldn't go as high in the section as Meres was unless you were – and his temper

on occasion was vicious: it was not a combination Brown Overcoat liked, so he went
back to headquarters by the shortest possible
route, and practised his excuses on the way.
When he reached the school he rang the bell
and the gross man admitted him without
question. He took off the brown overcoat as
he walked along the corridor to Meres' office
and became a person called Reynolds, a
former private detective, now a civil servant,
clerical grade, four weeks paid leave and
£1,750 per annum. When he reached the
office Reynolds had his first shock of the
evening: Jones wasn't there.

Meres, for Meres, was affable, and this
was the second shock. The fact that Callan
had shaken Reynolds didn't bother him at
all: if anything it had amused him. The fact
that Reynolds was unmarked he also found
amusing. And the fact that Jones had failed
to report in was the most amusing thing of
all. Cautiously, Reynolds began to try out
his excuses, but Meres stopped him with a
wave of his hand that was almost benign.

'Don't waste your eloquence,' he said.
'The chief wants to hear it too.'

And that was the third shock. Reynolds
had seen Hunter only three times in his life.
He followed Meres to the gloomy Ed-

64

wardian room, and told it all again. Out of his limitless patience Hunter listened, and then the questions began. How did Reynolds rate the man he had followed? How soon did the man become aware of him? How would he describe the little man his subject had talked to at The Peal of Bells? The one he himself had been sent to find? (This one had to be answered in nerve-wracking detail.) And how had the subject got away? Humiliating, this last, but Reynolds dared tell nothing but the truth. And still Meres smiled, and Hunter was patient as the story went on.

The subject, Reynolds said, was brilliant, and unquestionably a pro. There was no one in the section to match him. Here – and for the only time – Meres ceased to smile, but Hunter would allow no pause for recriminations. He had been on to them, Reynolds thought, before they even reached the tube station, and that made him outstanding. His evasive technique was first-class, and so was his nerve. Timing a jump through closing doors the way he had done demanded good reflexes and a lot of guts, even if the doors were supposed to stop when they touched you. There'd been a sureness about him too, almost a kind of cockiness: the way he'd winked for example when he'd wedged the telephone booth door. You had to be good to act that way. This was a big one: a number one.

But the bloke he'd met hadn't been like that at all. He'd been a small man in a small way of business, with neither the hope nor the ambition to be anything else. Almost Reynolds could have sympathized with the little bloke – if only he hadn't smelled so. But the smell didn't bother Hunter: it was even so to speak part of the pattern, though what the pattern was Reynolds had no idea. Even when he heard how the subject had trapped him, all Hunter said was, 'You were probably lucky, you know.'

And then, as if to prove it, there entered the biggest shock of all. Jones, wearing what looked at first like a grotesque purple moustache, that he finally recognized as a bruise smeared just below the tip of his nose. Then Reynolds realized just how lucky he had been.

Jones was young, ambitious, enthusiastic even. He knew his ability as a tail and was proud of it. Never in his life had he been taken with the lazy ease that this man had used, and the thought rankled, even hurt. He was dishevelled too, and the fact annoyed him. Jones liked to dress elegantly: his clothes were important to him.

'Even you were lucky,' Hunter said at last. 'He could have killed you if he'd wanted.'

'He bent my umbrella,' said Jones, as if that one gesture were worse, far worse than death.

Hunter said mildly, 'I think you're in a state of shock. Try to control it for just a little longer, and tell us how you would evaluate the subject. After that you can get some rest.'

Then Jones, like Reynolds before him, discovered what balm to wounded feelings there was in the fact that the subject had been brilliant, and rated him as high as Reynolds had done, or – he was the more enthusiastic of the pair – even higher. The knock-out chop he had received bothered him a little. Jones had done well in training exercises.

'The trouble is I wasn't ready for it,' he explained. 'If I had been–'

'If you had been he wouldn't have hit you in that particular way,' said Hunter. 'That is the whole point of this kind of fighting. To win. And the easiest way to do that is to take an unfair advantage. In our business, Jones, all advantages are unfair.'

'Yes, sir,' said Jones. His head ached abominably, but one question still bothered him. 'Do you know why he bent my umbrella–'

'He has a sense of humour,' said Hunter. 'It's a peculiar one, but apposite in its way. I think he realized that for you the umbrella may be a sort of symbol, and so he destroyed it.'

'Symbol of what, sir?'

Hunter shrugged. 'Elegance? Respectability? Power?'

'Manhood perhaps?' said Meres, very gently.

Jones subsided, but Reynolds had a question, and sufficient confidence to ask it.

'May we ask who the subject was, sir?'

'You may,' said Hunter. 'He's an operator attached to the section – for the moment. Your following him was in the nature of a training exercise. You didn't do too badly, all things considered, but I can hardly say that you did well. Either of you. You'd better go.'

When the door shut behind them, Hunter permitted himself a smile.

'So he's as good as ever,' he said.

'It seems like it, sir,' said Meres.

'I enjoyed your evaluation of the umbrella as a virility symbol,' Hunter said. 'Poor Jones. He was really quite gentle with him, all things considered. No one likes to be spied on, do they? That's why we're so unpopular.'

'It looks as if Callan's after another potency

symbol,' said Meres.

'A gun? Yes. I agree. There seems no other valid reason for him to look for that repellent little man. God knows one wouldn't do so from choice.'

Meres said, 'Guns are expensive, sir. Are you going to pay him for it?'

'No,' said Hunter. 'I'm not. Not till he uses it.'

'You still think he will, sir?'

'That may rather depend on your friends in the police force,' Hunter said.

'Hardly my friends, sir,' said Meres. He seemed shocked. 'They've got nothing to do with the Special Branch. I checked.'

'Then make them your friends. Persuade them – ever so gently, that they are *de trop.*' Hunter said.

CHAPTER FIVE

Callan went home feeling pretty good. Brown Overcoat and Rolled Umbrella had made his evening. They'd been a reminder, too, of how smart Hunter was. He'd guessed at once where Callan was going, and sent Brown Overcoat to wait for him there. That meant Hunter knew he was after a gun, which would at least help to convince him that he, Callan, was willing to go on with the job. And, Callan thought, maybe I am; I've had about as much of Waterman as I can take. But I'm not moving while there's rozzers about, and Hunter knows it. Ah well, the next move's up to him. He walked up to the flat, following the drill for the first time in months, doing it automatically and yet thoroughly, as if the section were still his whole life, cautious of the angle of the stairs, wary for shadows. The lock and key to his front door he had made himself, and they were the best. If anyone had tampered with the lock the key would tell him, and nobody had. He let himself in smoothly and easily, but without the appearance of haste, re-locked the door, hooked on the guard chain, then turned to examine his flat, the good mood dying in him, seeing it as Hunter might have done, or Meres even, looking at it for the first time. It wasn't a hell of a lot to show for thirty-four years of life, not when you considered the jobs he'd done, the blokes he'd killed. The section didn't pay you off in money for the jobs, or the blokes. You got a salary, and that was all. Some whimsically minded sod in the Treasury had decided that the going rate for an executioner was two hundred and six pounds five shillings and sevenpence a month, plus expenses. No pension fund. Even sods in the Treasury weren't as whimsically minded as that. He'd spent it as he'd got it. Booze and women, living like a gangster, and expecting to die like one, though he committed no crimes, merely broke the commandments... So every month he was broke, and he had this flat to prove it. This gaff. A poky bed-sitter, a kitchen like a cupboard, and a bath under the kitchen-table top, a loo that was a cockroach circus if you forgot the DDT powder just once. And even this lot cost too much money, but he clung on to it. It was the bath that kept him there. Old, slow and expensive to fill, it was nevertheless his bath. He shared it with nobody; and that was important. Ever since Malaya, Callan had been fanatically clean. Even in the nick.

He opened a tin of soup and set it to heat on a gas stove as old and inefficient as his bath, then turned to the table that housed his soldiers. He was busy with a squad of Prussians, the men who had fought the blueprint war against the French in 1870. Callan bought his soldiers unpainted. The painted ones cost too much money, and anyway he liked painting them himself. He picked up a Uhlan and examined it carefully. It was flawless. Horse and man blended into a fighting machine that really worked, even the lance a genuine weapon of war. The Uhlan's uniform was field-grey, the horse would be black, the lance brown with a silver tip. The Prussians had not regarded war as splendid or romantic; only necessary. It was the French, waiting in their boxes, who had gone in for splendour: scarlet, and blue, and gold. But the French had lost. Callan remembered the soup, switched off the stove just in time, then ate quickly, impatient to get back to his soldiers.

As he painted, Callan thought of Schneider, and how good he was, how secure in the knowledge of his own skill. One bullet could destroy all that, but the good ones like Schneider were able to see even one bullet coming, and step aside. That was why they were secure. It was never easy to take a Schneider, unless you were a madman. Nobody was safe against a nutter. They just stood right in front of you and blazed away, and what was going to happen next – and going to happen to *them* – never even crossed their minds. But Callan was a pro. Killing was often the least of his problems: the most urgent was escape. With two policemen already interested in Schneider, and himself working in the same building, escape would create its own problems, problems to which he dared not risk a solution. Callan had told the truth to Lonely: he was never going back inside – and for murder you got life. He put down the Uhlan and picked up an infantryman – field grey again, but with glistening jackboots. Schneider would have worn a uniform very like this one. He'd have been a good officer, Callan was sure, reducing his risks to a minimum, tackling them with skill and caution when they were unavoidable. Combat soldiers liked officers like that. They kept them alive.

I wonder what the hell he's done? Callan

thought, then remembered Schneider's invitation. 'Come and see my soldiers again. Whenever you like.'

Maybe he would do that. But he wouldn't wait for an invitation.

Meres hated to go to the Home Office. Its air of conscious rectitude depressed him, he despised its architecture and loathed its inhabitants: relaxed, purposeful, even content, some of them. Meres didn't like that at all, and so he took his victim to lunch. The victim in a sense chose himself: Eltringham had been to school with Meres, he was bright, successful – and he had the ear of his minister. Moreover he liked to eat: he was a very willing victim. When Meres had called him there had been no more than a token resistance: the magic word 'Caprice' saw to that.

Meres got there early and sipped campari and soda as he studied the menu, knowing that he would eat whatever Eltringham ordered: Eltringham invariably chose the best. The wine he would leave to the sommelier, but there would be lots of it. He wanted Eltringham mellow. Hunter was in a hurry, and Eltringham was by far his best hope to arrange things as they had to be arranged. Lunch at the Caprice was a small price to pay for that. He watched the door and Eltringham entered, twinkling, cherubic, already a little paunchy, but shrewd enough, and tough enough too, when he had to be. Meres suggested a dry martini, and Eltringham chose sherry. It wasn't, it seemed, going to be easy.

Over the smoked salmon, the caneton à l'orange and rum-babas they talked of school, the Brigade of Guards – in which they had both served – and women. Eltringham was knowledgeable on women: Meres was expert. With the salmon the sommelier suggested white burgundy, with the duck, Château Lascombes '59, and with the babas, Sauternes. Meres despised sweet wine, and left the Sauternes to Eltringham, who did not. When the coffee arrived, Meres suggested Bisquit, and Eltringham agreed. He bought Eltringham a cigar too, a Romeo y Julieta, and Eltringham's eyebrows rose. Carefully he warmed the brandy rummer in his cupped hands.

'My dear Toby,' he said, 'what a splendid expense account you must have.'

'Not at all. I'm paying for this myself,' Meres said.

Eltringham put down his brandy glass,

pierced and lit his cigar. That remark of Toby's was unfair, but then Toby had never done anything fairly in his life. Warily, he set out to discover what the fight was about.

'I wonder what I've done to deserve such generosity,' he said.

'Nothing – yet,' said Meres, and Eltringham winced. Not only unfair, but crude, too.

'Really, Toby,' he said. 'Is that what you say to your luscious popsies – once they get to the brandy?'

'My luscious popsies get Grand Marnier,' said Meres. 'It's quicker. And I never buy them château bottled claret. It's a waste of money.'

'And yet you bought it for me? My very dear Toby, I do hope you haven't wasted your money this time.'

'I hope so too,' said Meres, and Eltringham noted and filed in his memory the silken menace of his voice. 'Let's find out.' Eltringham waited.

'It's the police,' said Meres. 'They're being a nuisance.'

'So often they are,' said Eltringham. 'Did they make you blow into one of those turgid little bags?'

Meres made an abrupt and angry gesture, and Eltringham noticed how powerful his hands were, despite their elegance.

'I'm talking about my trade,' he said. 'My very dubious trade.'

'But I thought you weren't allowed to do that,' said Eltringham. 'Official Secrets Act and all that.'

'This is an emergency,' said Meres.

'I thought your whole life was an emergency. And anyway you must forgive me, my knowledge of your activities derives from the cinema – but don't you get issued with awful warnings? You know – "Good luck Caruthers old man, but I must remind you that if your activities come to the notice of the authorities we can do nothing to help you. You're on your own." Don't tell me they don't actually *say* that. I should be so disappointed.'

'They say it all right,' said Meres. 'And they mean it.'

'Well then–'

'We have a job on,' said Meres. 'We've got clearance for it. From the top.' At once Eltringham dropped the airy manner. 'The trouble is our subject's got involved with the police. They're chivvying him a bit. You know the sort of thing. And it's as good as a bodyguard. We can't get near him.'

'What do you want to do to him?'

Meres hesitated as a waiter scurried by.

'Kill him,' he said.

Eltringham said, 'I rather wish I hadn't asked.' Meres shrugged. 'It isn't really Home Office business, you know.'

'It's from the top,' said Meres. 'At the moment all I'm doing is asking–'

'May one know why? I mean it's so un-typical,' Eltringham said.

'We like to keep it light,' said Meres. 'That way the police don't get *too* interested. Of course I could put in an official request–'

Eltringham shuddered. 'Please don't,' he said. 'What is it you want?' He hesitated, then added. 'I should prefer a minimum of detail.'

'Get Detective Inspector Pollard and Detective Sergeant Grace off the Hong Kong inquiry,' said Meres. 'Temporarily. For a week at the most.'

'And that's all?'

'That's all.'

'You will let me know when they will be able to resume?'

'I will.'

Eltringham admired the slow growth of ash on his cigar.

'I think that can be arranged,' he said. 'As it's from the top, I mean.'

Meres was silent, and Eltringham continued, 'Will you – er – deal with the subject?'

'You've no business to ask that,' said Meres. 'And you know it. But I'll answer it anyway. No, I shan't. Not this time.'

'I wish I didn't have to know about you,' said Eltringham.

'Somebody has to. And you're such splendid cover. What more natural than our lunching together? A couple of old school pals.' Eltringham winced.

'Why so unhappy?' said Meres. 'If you handle this properly it could do you quite a bit of good.'

Eltringham said, 'I'd already thought of that.'

That day Callan kept away from Schneider. Schneider was in trouble, and Callan wanted no part of it. The lessons he'd learned in the Scrubs paid off. There were police all over the place, and Schneider was the one they watched. Coppers. Rozzers. Filth. They had all sorts of names, but once you'd done bird you learned to spot them first, before they spotted you, the big men in raincoats who had all the time in the world to watch and wait. This time they made no effort to hide what they were, and Callan kept out of their

79

way and bickered with Waterman and drank a half of bitter with his lunch while his nerves screamed for whisky.

It was Friday, pay-day, and Waterman made him wait for it. He always did. Going to the bank was far too good an opportunity to be rushed. Banks, like pubs, didn't close till three... At three-thirty he appeared at Callan's elbow, and Callan endured again the smell of gin and mixed pickles. Slowly, laboriously, Waterman counted out two five-pound notes, four one-pound notes, four half crowns, a sixpence and two ha'pennies. Callan went on working.

'It's all there,' Waterman said.

'You should get me a microscope,' said Callan. 'I could see it better.'

'It's more than you deserve,' said Waterman. 'And anyway – business is bad.'

'Don't tell me,' said Callan. 'I'm your book-keeper.'

'It'll get worse,' said Waterman. 'I'll have to start cutting down.'

'Gin's far too expensive,' Callan said. 'You should switch to meths.'

Dyspepsia stabbed at Waterman, and his temper exploded.

'I'm fed up with your insolence,' he yelled. 'You're fired. You hear me?'

'The whole bloody building can hear you,' said Callan.

'You can finish what you're doing and get out,' Waterman said. The pork pie stabbed again, and his fingers went to his stomach, solicitous.

'I'm ill,' he said, 'I'm in pain. But you don't care, do you? Nobody cares. All right then. You can get stuffed. *Everybody* can get stuffed. I'm off to the chemist.' He stormed to the door. 'I don't want you here when I get back.' The door slammed.

Callan stared at the figures in front of him. He'd done it this time. He was fired – and he'd lost his chance with Hunter. No use apologizing to Waterman either, not in this mood. He'd ordered him out even quicker... He picked up his pen again, and worked on till six. Waterman didn't return and there was no call from Charlie. At six exactly he quit. The desk contained nothing that was his. All he had to do was put on his coat and leave. It should have been good to leave.

On the way out, Schneider passed him, moving in long, impatient strides to the detective waiting outside. Schneider seemed angry, but the anger was both single-minded and controlled. He passed Callan without seeing him, but when he spoke to the detective he neither shouted nor blustered.

'My friend,' he said, 'I am now going home. If you persist in following me I cannot stop you, but I must warn you I shall call the police.'

He walked on down the road, and a Daimler Conquest whispered to a stop beside him. Schneider got in the back and Callan watched the car go by. It was not the car he would have expected Schneider to own, not at first, and then, as he thought about it, it was. The Daimler had all the casual elegance that Schneider worked at so hard in his clothes, his manners, his uneasily handled upper class English speech. And like Schneider, the firm of Daimler was German in origin. Schneider's chauffeur looked English enough, big and lean and competent: a man to approach with caution – but his uniform was field grey. Callan wondered if, like his master, he had learned to use a gun, then watched as the detective went to find a telephone and report failure.

Callan walked down the street to a bus stop, and rain began to fall, small, spiteful rain that reminded him how cold it was, how much he needed a new raincoat. Five minutes went by, and the detective joined the bus queue. He didn't look like a man who had just reported failure: he looked like a man who had been told he could go home early. In spite of the rain, he seemed happy. When Callan left the bus he was still on it, and still happy. Callan was not. He had lost two jobs in one day, and that was enough. On the other hand, he no longer had to kill Schneider, and that was a cause for happiness. Callan stopped at the off-licence and invested some of his wages in a half bottle of whisky.

CHAPTER SIX

He'd had a couple of stiff ones when he heard the knock on the door. For a moment he panicked, and then he remembered. Lonely. Seven o'clock. All the same... He turned the door handle and pulled back the door, leaving the guard chain on. It was Lonely. He was taking the chain off when the door behind Lonely opened and Miss Brewis came out. Nice old love, Miss Brewis. Cheerful. Always a kind word. But nosy. Dead nosy.

'Yes?' said Callan.

Lonely heard the footsteps behind him.

'Mr. Callan?' he said.

'Yes?'

'Got a parcel for you,' said Lonely.

Miss Brewis said 'Goodnight' and walked on. Parcels for Callan could only mean one thing: those ridiculous soldiers he played with. Really, men were such children – though this one had ever such a nice smile. The thought of Callan's smile kept Miss Brewis warm all the way to the pictures.

Callan waited till the footsteps faded, then

pushed the door open. Lonely scuttled inside.

'Let's have a look,' said Callan. Lonely put the parcel on the table and Callan opened it. Brown paper on top, then newspaper, then oily rags. A box of heavy cardboard – ammo – and the gun. It was a Smith and Wesson Airweight right enough. He opened the breach, squinted down the barrel, tested its balance. A nice gun. Nice balance. Accurate too... Lonely marvelled at the quick precision of his hands.

'I'm sorry, Lonely old sport, but it won't do,' Callan said.

'Something wrong, Mr. Callan?'

'Not with the gun,' said Callan. 'It's perfect. I haven't got a hundred quid.'

'I could carry you for a day or two, Mr. Callan.'

'I might need a bit longer than that,' Callan said, and Lonely's face fell. 'Thanks anyway.'

He wrapped up the parcel again, and Lonely took it reluctantly.

'This'll be bad for you, won't it?' Callan said.

'No. I'll tell the geezer I couldn't find you,' Lonely said, then hesitated. 'You sure you're all right, Mr. Callan? I can manage a few quid.'

Callan looked round the room. 'Worse than the nick, isn't it?' The look he gave the little man was gentle. 'Go on home, Lonely. Scarper.'

The little man was at the door when Callan said, 'Where can I find you?' Lonely gave him an address, and Callan's lips moved: he didn't write it down. The way things were going he might be glad of a friend. Even Lonely.

Next day was Saturday, and for once he didn't have to break his neck getting over to the City. He could spend Saturday morning the way all the sensible people did. In bed. He got out once, made coffee and toast, then got back in again. With him he took Sir Charles Oman's *History of the Peninsular War*. Even Hunter couldn't get past Wellington. He read for a solid two hours, and his coffee was cold when the knock sounded on the door. Not a timid knock, like Lonely's. This geezer wanted to get in. Callan struggled into his faded dressing-gown and slippers and pulled the door back on its chain.

'Mr. Waterman,' he said. 'This is a surprise.'

'I want to talk to you, Callan,' Waterman said.

'Of course.'

Quietly, unseen, Callan unhooked the chain and opened the door. Something good was going to happen. He knew it. Waterman entered, and Callan took what was left of the whisky and put it in a cupboard. Waterman took it without a blink.

'By rights you should work a week's notice,' he said.

'By rights you should pay me a week's wages,' said Callan. 'Anyway – you told me to get out.'

'Maybe I was a bit hasty,' Waterman said. 'I was ill. I *told* you I was ill.'

Even when he comes to plead he starts yelling, Callan thought.

'So what can I do for you?' he asked.

'There's a lot of new orders. Urgent. Come in this morning,' Waterman said. 'I've got to have them checked by Monday.'

'It'll ruin your weekend,' said Callan.

'I can't cope. I'm ill,' Waterman said.

You've got a bird, Callan thought. Randy old sod.

'I speak hasty sometimes,' said Waterman. 'I do. I admit it. I'm my own worst enemy.' He paused, and added, 'The office was hell this morning.'

'Do you – want me back?' said Callan.

'Yes. I do,' Waterman yelled.

'Same wages?'

'Ten bob more, if you come in this afternoon.'

'Make it a quid, and I'll come in all day tomorrow. I got a lot on today.'

Waterman yelled a bit more, but he gave in the end. He had no choice, and anyway he liked yelling.

After that Callan was feeling pretty good, until he went out that afternoon to do his shopping. When he came back Miss Brewis was at her door. She held a circular in her hand and Callan saw that he had got one too. He pulled it out of his letterbox. It was for a new detergent.

'I see you've got one,' said Miss Brewis, and came over to him. '"Sheer". I've never heard of it.'

'What are they giving away this time?'

'Plastic goldfish,' said Callan. His voice was dull.

'How extraordinary,' Miss Brewis said.

'No food, no mess, no drama,' said Callan. 'They don't live, so they can't die.'

'There's a red spot on the corner of yours,' said Miss Brewis, who had no taste for romantic irony. 'I wonder what that means?'

'It means I get a chance for the bonus,' said Callan. 'If I want to take it. Bye bye,

Miss Brewis.'

'Bye bye,' Miss Brewis said. She sounded disappointed. She always was disappointed when Callan was moody.

Callan went inside his flat and dialled the special number. The relief secretary answered, and Callan wondered, for the hundredth time, what Hunter's secretary did on her day off, and who she did it with.

'Charlie speaking,' said Hunter. So the scrambler would be on.

'I got your message,' Callan said. 'Why couldn't you phone me?'

'I wanted you to see the colour red,' said Hunter. 'I thought it might remind you of something.'

'Not when the police are around. I told you,' Callan said.

'Toby has attended to that. They won't be in your way, I promise.'

So that was it then. The job was on again. If Hunter said 'I promise', that really was it. Callan looked at the hand that held the telephone. It was shaking.

'Well?' said Hunter.

'There's another little complication,' Callan said. 'I'm skint.'

'Indeed?'

'Indeed is right, and guns cost money.'

There was a pause. Hunter would be thinking. His face would show nothing but its inevitable, nailed-on patience, but his mind would be racing.

'The job pays a bonus,' he said at last. 'One hundred pounds. You can have it in advance – today. I'll send a man round.'

The bastard knew everything.

'You mustn't spoil me,' said Callan. 'With a hundred quid I'll break even.'

He hung up and went back to his Prussian soldiers, but they had no power to intrigue him. Hunter still wasn't sure of him; and the knowledge was bitter – and frightening. If Hunter had been sure he'd have offered Callan a section gun, and they were un-traceable. Guns bought for a hundred quid were all too traceable, especially when you knew who the supplier was – as Hunter would.

On Sunday he went to the office to get Waterman out of the mess he'd made. It was a cold day, with the threat of rain, so that the raincoat was quite appropriate – and useful too. It had a special pocket that Callan had sewn in himself, a long, narrow pocket just wide enough to take the replica of the kit of tools he'd designed and made for his try at the supermarket safe. They were good tools, and so was the wallet that held them; a handsome piece of work done in compartments, the leather padded so that the metal couldn't chink. Callan had bought it at Harrods one Christmas. It was supposed to hold the chromium plated spanners the rich bought when they wanted to tinker with their Aston-Martins...

Waterman had left the place in a mess. Cheques, letters and invoices all over the place. Callan scowled, as he always did when confronted with the evidence of Waterman's untidiness. It was greed that drove the man on: the only money-making talent he possessed. He pressed the wad of five-pound notes in his inside pocket. If Waterman knew it was there, he wouldn't rest till he'd got his hands on it. On the other hand, Callan thought, I'm going to get the means to defend myself, Mr. Waterman. A Smith and Wesson 38 Airweight, and Christ help me when it goes off.

He set to work, and slowly order came from chaos, entries were posted, accounts balanced. As always, Callan found that, in a gentle way, he liked what he was doing: liked the sense of something being made to work. The morning went by in the City's Sunday silence, and nothing destroyed the intensity of his concentration. By one o'clock the work was half-over. Callan took a breather and rubbed his eyes that ached from deciphering Waterman's vile figures and viler script. It was at times like these that he wished he smoked. But smoking was out, for him. It made him cough too easily. And coughing at the wrong time could kill you. He stood up and stretched, easing the cramp out of his muscles, then took the wallet of tools from his raincoat and put on a pair of thin cotton gloves. Suddenly his hand stabbed down, came up in a blur of speed holding his pen, pointing it, pretending it was a gun. But now wasn't the time for guns, even if he were going to look in on Schneider. Guns would come later, maybe, once he'd had some practice and found out what it was that Schneider had done. It was all very well for Hunter sitting there in a school full of junk, looking at maps and giving orders, but Callan was the one who pulled the trigger, and sometimes got shot at in return. And when it came to that kind of jeopardy, Callan liked to know why, even if Hunter said he mustn't. Hunter had brains all right; but he couldn't feel.

The building was deserted: it had to be.

Schneider's office was a damn difficult place to burgle. Unless you were good, it was an impossible place to burgle. Callan was good, but it took time. First there was the lock itself. Parkinson's had made it, and it was a good one. The simplest thing to do was to cut round it, but that wasn't on. Nobody must know he'd been. So he probed and measured with calipers, spread newspaper on the floor – the *News of the World*, that kept him in touch with old friends – and cut and filed at a piece of blank steel. That was where the time went. The steel had to be tempered: mild steel would bend inside the lock and the wards wouldn't turn. But it was satisfying work, that demanded all of his skill and flair – and forty minutes later, the door opened an inch or two. Callan held it still then, and reached out with a long piece of telescopic steel, found the switch of a burglar alarm and pressed it down. At last it was safe to go inside.

'Schneider,' Callan called. 'Are you there, old love?'

But Schneider was wherever rich men spend their Sundays, buying expensive drinks for expensive women. 'It is right that you should be exploited,' Schneider had said. 'I'm a capitalist myself.' But capital too has its problems, Mr. Schneider. Callan shut the door behind him.

It was a nice office, three times as big as Callan's; the furniture worth a hundred times whatever Waterman had paid for the wood and metal scrap Callan used. He looked at the table full of soldiers, then began to search the office. It was apparent at once that Schneider was untidy on the grand scale. Invoices cascaded on the desk, sprang up from drawers when Callan opened them. And such harmless invoices. Cameras, tape-recorders, bicycles, tins of fruit. Callan looked at hundreds of them, and could find no reason why Hunter should wish Schneider dead. He tried every drawer in the desk – none of them was locked – and found nothing; he searched for a secret hiding-place. There was none. Next the filing cabinet. That was locked, but his tools opened it at once. Inside each drawer were more invoices, orders, correspondence: great wadded masses like a filing-clerk's nightmare. Callan reckoned that Schneider must carry all his essential information in his head. It would take weeks to bring order out of this chaos – and such innocent chaos. He looked under the carpet, behind the radiator, the pelmet of the curtains. Nothing. Schneider was simply a very messy, very rich man – whom Hunter wanted dead. Callan went on searching. Somewhere in the room there had to be a reason why Schneider had to die: why the police followed him till Hunter warned them off. He sat down on the chair to think, and the whoopee cushion sounded a raspberry. Callan jumped, then looked at the chair and picked it up. 'Very droll,' he said. He pushed his gloved hand down the back of Schneider's leather chair. Something thin and hard met his fingers. He eased it out carefully. A visiting card, elegant and narrow. 'Rudolf Schneider' it said and a Hampstead address and telephone number. 'Where else?' said Callan, and groped again in the bran tub. Something else was there, but it took the telescopic rod to get it out. A key. A hand-made key for a hand-made lock. The kind he himself had once made. A key that fitted no lock in the office. Callan put the key in his pocket. It was time he made another.

He looked at his watch. Two-thirty and he still had those damned accounts to finish. He was hungry too: but commerce and hunger must wait. Surely to God this room had something else to tell him? He thought hard about Schneider. Ageing but hard, pleased with life, secure in his own resources. Rich. The office proved it, his clothes proved it, his car proved it. But you don't get rich when you treat your orders the way Schneider treated his, with the kind of carelessness that was either contemptuous or insane. Not unless, like Waterman, you had a Callan to clear up after you: and Schneider worked alone. He went to the table where the soldiers were, the only area in the room that was orderly, neat, even precise. But it was just a table, no drawers, no hiding places, the soldiers expensively moulded lead, no more. He picked up the gun-carriage, his best and final chance. That was solid too, but the barrel of the gun was hollow. He shook it, and something rattled inside. He probed again with the thin steel rod, and a stub of pencil slid on to his cupped palm, rolled and was still. Printed on the pencil was one word: Noguchi.

It took him three seconds to remember where he had seen that word. It had been on the butt of a gun at Hunter's HQ, a magnum revolver, 38 calibre. A good gun, accurate. Callan never ignored good, accurate guns, nor did Hunter: nor, it seemed, did Schneider. He dropped the pencil back in the gun-barrel, then studied the room, concentrating on it a section at a time. It was exactly as it had been when he came in. Carefully, he opened the door a fraction and listened. There was no one about as he stepped on to the threshold, switched on the burglar alarm and shut the door, feeling the lock grip hard. He went back to the accounts in his office, and by five o'clock he was finished. There was a masochistic pleasure in looking at the neatly arranged desk that Waterman would demolish next day. Callan went into Waterman's office, and looked in the L to R directory. There was nothing under Noguchi. He tried the classified: Firearms, Gunsmiths, Arms Manufacturers. Nothing. But he had a hundred quid, and the Noguchi was a likely gun. It mightn't be a bad idea to have a word with Lonely before the pubs opened.

This time Lonely was in Notting Hill. He moved around a lot. The police – and his enemies, real and imagined – made that essential. In any case the nomadic life suited Lonely. He preferred it. The only fixed points in his existence were prisons... Callan sat in the tube and read the *News of the World*. The news, and the world, were as nasty as ever. Birth, copulation and death. An education officer had once read them a poem about that. It made more sense than the stupid gits in this paper. Off their heads by the sound of them, or maybe they're just bored. Like you, Callan, he told himself. You're bored mate. And look at the mess you're getting into.

He left the tube at Kensington High Street and went through the drill, but nobody was following him. The street lay emptied by Sunday rain, and sensible people stayed at home, made love and watched the telly, and waited for the pubs to open. Callan walked to Church Street and got wet, then waited in a doorway for a bus that splashed him as he hurried out to meet it. The bus conductor was from Barbados, and he sang a song about rum. It was a cheerful song, but the bus conductor was miserable. Callan left the bus near Notting Hill tube station, and the bus conductor stood on the platform and went on singing. Suddenly Callan felt a stab of hatred as intense as pain. It was a hatred of himself. He began to walk quickly, working out this alien, dangerous emotion, feeling the rain seep through his coat and dull the edge of his hate. There was a cafeteria near Lonely's place, and he queued and bought tea, sausages, a pie and chips, then sat down to eat among people as solitary as himself. There'd been a piece in the paper about that the other day. 'London is full of lonely people.' He bet the geezer who'd written that hadn't been lonely. Probably got a wife and three kids and a mother-in-law and a mortgage to stop him feeling that way ever again. But he'd been right, even so. London was full of lonely people, and what the hell could you do about it?

The loneliest of all lived in the sort of condemned area that fitted him the way a sty fits a pig. He had the attic in a sagging Victorian barrack that had been carved up into 'single rooms'. Not even a house agent had the nerve to call them flatlets. Callan climbed the stairs past the sounds of Sunday: Radio One and cathode-ray cowboys and kids yelling and a good old-fashioned family punch-up, and at the top, Lonely's room. He knocked, and the voice inside said, 'Who is it?' at once. Even in the three words, Callan could taste the fear.

'It's me,' he said. 'Callan.'

The door opened, and Lonely stood warily inside, then threw it wide.

'Come in, Mr. Callan,' he said, and the fear was still there, but now it was a familiar fear, almost a welcome one, compared with the fear of the unknown.

Callan went inside and stood, hands in pockets, looking round the room.

'Jesus,' he said.

Lonely shuffled defensively.

'I wasn't expecting visitors, Mr. Callan. If I was I'd have tidied the place up a bit,' he said.

The room looked like an antique shop dedicated to esoteric rubbish. There was junk piled in corners, spread out on tables, seeping out from under the unmade bed: all kinds of junk, its only common denominator a total lack of commercial value. One wall was almost obscured by a moth-eaten flag of the USSR, broken plaster casts of Michelangelo's David and the Medici Venus stood on either side of the fireplace, an ancient horn gramophone stood *in* the fireplace, its spring uncoiled like a striking serpent. An enormous deal table was obscured by aspidistras, chamberpots, Coronation mugs and jam jars, an orange box in the middle of the room was crammed full with pieces of jigsaw puzzles, there was an almost bald bearskin rug on the floor and a stuffed leopard, much bothered by mildew, in the corner. On the mantelshelf were eleven clocks, all with one or both hands missing, and on pegs over the door a fireman's helmet without a strap, a pickelhaube devoured by rust and a pearly queen's hat with a broken ostrich feather hung in neat alignment. The stuff from under the bed, like flotsam washed up by the tide, seemed to be mostly the kind of artificial flowers that were once put round graves under cloches.

'Did you – did you thieve all this?'

Even to himself, Callan's voice sounded hysterical, and he accepted Lonely's look of scorn almost with relief.

'Course not,' Lonely said. This isn't my gaff, Mr. Callan. It's me cousin Alfred's. He's a bit eccentric.'

'I can see he must be,' said Callan. 'Where's he now?'

'Totting,' said Lonely. 'Over in Ponder's End. He kips over the garage where he keeps his lorry. Alfred says there's a lot of old birds there got marvellous junk.'

'Looks as if he's collected most of it,' said Callan.

'He likes junk, Alfred does,' said Lonely.

'Blimey, he must do,' said Callan.

He put his hand into his inside pocket and brought out the five pound notes.

'Count them,' he said, and Lonely did so with a bank clerk's smooth dexterity.

'A hundred quid exactly, Mr. Callan,' he said.

'And what can you buy for a hundred quid?'

'Your shooter? But I took it back, Mr. Callan.' The little man looked terrified. 'You said you didn't want it.'

'I said I couldn't afford it,' said Callan. 'Now I can.'

The terror stayed with Lonely – Callan could smell it, but something else was added to it now: admiration, even awe.

'You knocked off a hundred quid, Mr. Callan?'

'I needed a gun,' Callan said. 'You're going to get me one.'

'Smith and Wesson Airweight and a hundred rounds. He's still got it, Mr. Callan.'

'Ask him if he's got a Noguchi Magnum 38 calibre instead,' said Callan.

'Noguchi?' Lonely made the word a question, and Callan nodded. 'Foreign is it?'

'Yeah,' said Callan. 'Foreign. But accurate, Lonely, I could shoot you in the dark with it son. Just aim at the middle of the smell.'

'I can't help it, Mr. Callan,' the little man said. 'You scare me.'

'I should,' said Callan. 'Sometimes I scare myself. So keep your mouth shut.'

Lonely began to protest then, but the protest was interrupted by a rhythmic metallic banging. Lonely stood frozen in horror, then dashed to a cupboard and rummaged frantically.

'What the hell is it?' said Callan.

'Bogeys in the street,' Lonely said. 'The first one that sees them bangs on the water pipes.'

'You been thieving?' Callan asked. 'The truth, mind.' Lonely nodded. 'Right. We better get out of here. I don't want the rozzers reclaiming my hundred quid.'

Lonely emerged from the cupboard holding a length of rope.

'The skylight, is it?' asked Callan.

Lonely nodded again, and Callan stood on the table and unhooked the skylight latch. It opened without a sound. Lonely passed him the rope, and Callan latched one knotted end to a hook driven into the skylight frame, then swarmed up and on to the roof. Below, Lonely, moving at frantic speed, put on a raincoat and rammed a transistor radio and a set of silver-plated fishknives in its pockets, then shot up the rope like a monkey. Callan coiled the rope as Lonely lowered the skylight into place, then they moved softly, swiftly across the leads. Below them was an empty police car and a bunch of kids, the only ones who had seen them. None of the kids shouted, none, after the first glance, even looked up. They reached a gable end, and the comparative shelter of an adjoining street. Behind them, Callan thought he heard the sound of a fist on a door. So did Lonely. He went down a drainpipe, fishknives clinking, as if gravity had no meaning. Callan followed, more warily, then the two of them walked through the slow-drying streets until the sounds of a police siren made Lonely restless again. He wanted to run, but Callan made him slow down, following a group of the elderly righteous with hymn books in their hands, who led him to a nonconformist chapel, and sanctuary, and the shelter from the wind, till the pubs opened. They were crossing its threshold when the police car went past, and from then on Lonely began to feel secure, bawling his way through 'Onward Christian Soldiers' and The Old Rugged Cross'.

'Just like being back in the Scrubs, Mr. Callan,' he whispered. He even enjoyed the sermon. It was about the lusts of the flesh.

Afterwards Callan took him to a pub and bought him a pie and a couple of pints of beer while he himself drank one slow, cautious whisky. The pub was big and noisy, full of desperate Sunday drinkers, and far away from Notting Hill.

'I'm ever so grateful, Mr. Callan,' Lonely said.

'Then get me that gun.'

'If you say so, Mr. Callan.'

'I do say so.'

Lonely said, 'Look, Mr. Callan. I know it's none of my business, but supposing you killed somebody with it?'

'Then he'd be dead, wouldn't he?' said Callan. 'What d'you think I want a gun for anyway? Cowboys and Indians?'

'It's just – I like you, Mr. Callan. You've been a good friend to me. I don't want to see you get hurt.'

'I won't get hurt,' said Callan. 'Not if you get me the gun.'

Lonely sighed. 'I'll do my best, Mr. Callan.'

'That's all right then,' Callan said. 'Where are you going to sleep tonight?'

'Me Aunty Mildred'll give me a kip,' said Lonely.

'Is she bent too?'

'Aunt Mildred? No. She used to be on the batter. She's got pots of money.'

Callan finished his whisky.

'Bring the thing to my flat,' he said. 'And get rid of those fishknives for Gawd's sake. You're clanking like a freight yard.'

CHAPTER SEVEN

On Sundays Schneider always felt good. It was such a very English day, and now that he was so very English, too, he had almost got the hang of it. Even the phrase 'got the hang of it' proved it. He smiled. Schneider enjoyed being English, but it was necessary for him, too. At least it was necessary for him to find a new nationality. Never again could he be a German. And so he was English, because they were such a delightful people. Consider this Sunday business. It was boredom raised to a fine art. A long yawn over breakfast and the papers, beer in a pub, then a prescribed lunch of roast beef, roast potatoes, mashed potatoes, carrots and greens, and – for the cook – a nerve-wracking struggle with a Yorkshire pudding that could be either disaster or delight, the one Sunday landmark that wasn't boring. Then after lunch, bed with one's wife or mistress, and for most Englishmen that too seemed an aspect of boredom, perhaps because of their idealization of the national state of mind known as 'muddling through'.

Schneider was as ready and willing to muddle through as the next Englishman, but not in bed. Not with Jenny.

For Schneider Jenny would always be a problem: a maddening, bewildering, utterly adorable problem. She was twenty-three years old, slender, unobtrusively beautiful: his confidential secretary and mistress. Lovable secretary, hyper-efficient mistress. Jenny was his filing system, his wife, his child, the only woman in a long procession of women that Schneider had failed first to comprehend, then dominate, then reject. The only one he had loved, and continued to love, until now just to be with her was enough, and he never wanted to comprehend her: wished only that the beautiful enigma should go on being enigmatic. Even in bed. Even on Sunday afternoon. He loved her with a passionate lack of control that had at first frightened, then delighted him, but never had he been able to gauge her body's responses by his own. There was a final tranquillity about her that nothing could pierce, and for this too Schneider loved her. He recognized the irony of his situation, but it delighted him also, and even increased his love. For now Schneider was rich and respectable, very close to the target of a quarter of a million sterling, the basic minimum he had set himself for retirement in what he had learned to call moderate comfort, and Jenny was a Chinese whore he had bought out of a Hong Kong brothel in the spring of 1964.

He lay beside her, as she slept on her stomach, and ran his hand gently down from her shoulders, over her back, her small firm buttocks. The rhythmical contact made her as relaxed as a cat, and Schneider took pride in the utter trust of her untroubled sleep. For the thousandth time he sought for the words that would describe her body's colour and texture: golden – saffron – bronze: silk over velvet. The words were there, but it would take a poet to arrange them into an order worthy of her. Schneider was no poet, but there was pleasure even in this struggle for poetry. She stirred under his hands – a tiny movement – then came awake at once as she always did, her body flexed and she rolled into his arms. Schneider looked at her neat little breasts, their nipples rich as rubies, then down to the flatness of her delicately dimpled belly. She put one hand up under his chin, and smiled at him, the brown eyes tender, then her other hand moved, the smile widened to a grin as she snuggled beneath him, her body gave way to a tiny trembling as he took her once more. When he had done – was she, too, satisfied? Had he fulfilled her? Schneider would never know – she pushed him over on to his back, lay with her head on his shoulder.

'You make me very happy,' said Jenny, and Schneider knew it was true, just as he knew this was part of their Sunday ritual, part of the joy she gave him.

'Why do I make you happy?' he asked. It was the question she insisted upon.

'Because you love me the way a woman wants to be loved.'

'And which way is that?'

'With strength,' said Jenny, 'but also with tenderness. But most of all with joy because it's me.'

Suddenly her hand flicked out, she nipped him in the thigh, and Schneider yelled.

'You have stopped thinking about me. You are thinking of something else.' She was never wrong about this. 'What are you thinking about?'

Schneider said, 'I'm thinking about a young man named Callan.'

'Is he prettier than me?' Jenny asked. He felt her fingers move.

'No,' said Schneider. 'Nobody is.' The

threatened pinch became a caress. 'Callan is a madman. Like me. He plays the war game.' The caress continued.

'He is a very clever young man,' said Schneider, 'but he is also uneducated, and a failure. I think he would play the war game very well. One day I may ask him here and find out.' Her hand stopped moving.

'Is that all you want from him?' she asked.

'What else could there be?'

'I thought perhaps you were looking for an assistant.'

'I have an assistant. You. But you're not assisting me at the moment.' Her hand refused to move. 'I have you to remember things, and George to drive the car. Why should I need anyone else?'

'To make more money,' said Jenny.

'Money is very important,' Schneider said.

'So is being alive. Being alive is even more important than money.'

'We're alive,' said Schneider, 'and when we have enough money we'll stop making more – but we won't stop living.'

'I do not think that day will ever come,' said Jenny.

'I do,' said Schneider. 'I think it will come soon.'

He put his fingers over hers, and her hand

began to move again.

Lonely hated this gun business. He hated the man who sold them, he hated having to carry the thing through the streets, he hated handing it over to Mr. Callan. (Even in his thoughts, Callan was always Mr. Callan to Lonely.) The only bit of bunce in the whole deal was the money. For a ride in a bus and back, carrying the thing, Lonely's share in the transaction was ten per cent. Ten nicker for a couple of bus rides – good money that, except a rozzer might stop him and ask him what he was carrying. Rozzers were like that. Flaming nosy. Out for promotion – and with a shooter on you they could put you down for ten years. Then there was the bloke you had to go and buy it from. The Greek, they called him. No Christian name. No surname. Just the Greek. A geezer who smiled at you all the time and made funny jokes in some weird language that sounded like chewing peanuts. But it wasn't the jokes Lonely minded. The Greek terrified Lonely, and Lonely hated him for the fear.

He got off the bus at Sloane Street and walked along Knightsbridge, full of the bustling rich looking for things to spend their money on even if it *was* Monday. He watched a woman coming out of a dress shop, stuffing a fat purse into a crocodile leather handbag: an American with a roll of money in his hip pocket so fat he looked as if he'd got a carbuncle on his backside. Either one of them would have been dead easy, but Mr. Callan had said no slip-ups, and if you had any sense you always did what Mr. Callan told you. But to let the money stay where it was...

It isn't fair, thought Lonely. It isn't bleeding fair.

He passed two minks and a leopardskin, then turned off the main road into a lonely square, dodged among the Bentleys and Jensens, and turned off again into a mews, an unassuming row of eighteenth-century cottages that had once been just about good enough for the servants, and now were far too good for the masters. The Greek had a house facing a yard leading off from the mews. All he showed to the world was a rather battered door fitted with a bell and a loudspeaker. Lonely pressed the bell. Already his hands were sweating, and he knew he smelled.

'Yes?' said the speaker. The Greek's voice, bored, uncaring, and insolent with the insolence of a man who has successfully abolished fear from his life.

'It's me,' Lonely said into the speaker. 'Lonely.'

'Oh, God,' said the voice. 'I suppose you'd better come in.'

The buzzer whirred, and after a moment the door opened slightly. Lonely went into the yard beyond, careful to close the door behind him. The yard was elegant with flowers in gaudy pots and shrubs in varnished barrels that would have cost Lonely a week's rent. He went up to the mahogany door and passed inside, wondering how the Greek would receive him this time. Once he'd been stark naked under a sun-lamp, once he'd been on the sofa with a bird, once he'd been in bed with a feller, but always the Greek had made him nervous, and not knowing a name you could call out made it worse. You couldn't call out 'Greek!' Not to this geezer. Lonely coughed loudly, and hoped, without conviction, for the best.

'I'm here,' the Greek said, and Lonely made his way to the kitchen.

It was a splendid kitchen, all white and gleaming steel like an operating theatre, and the Greek was all in white too, bleeding Kildare thought Lonely, treating a steak like it was a busted appendix or something. The Greek spared Lonely one glance, then concentrated on his fillet, waiting for the exact degree of brownness before he transferred it to a plate that already contained french beans that smelt elusively of something like onion. Garlic, Lonely thought. That's what it is... Bloody foreigners – mucking up good food. The Greek poured himself a glass of red wine and began to eat. The steak melted off the knife but Lonely was too frightened to feel hunger. He stood, not daring to sit, while the Greek finished the steak and beans, drank wine, then selected an apple from a bowl and crunched into it. His teeth were white, regular and very strong.

At last the Greek said, 'Lonely, how nice of you to call. Tell me. How may I serve you?'

'It's about a shooter,' Lonely said.

'The one you brought back? Has your friend changed his mind?'

'I told you I couldn't find him–' Lonely began.

'You lied. It is not important.'

'He doesn't fancy the Smith and Wesson anyway.'

'What does he fancy?'

'Noguchi,' said Lonely. 'Centre-fire magnum revolver .38 calibre.' He said it as a child might repeat the memorized words of a language it does not understand.

'Noguchi?' said the Greek. 'What does your friend find so special about a Noguchi?'

'He just said he fancied it,' said Lonely.

'A gun is not a bird, Lonely,' said the Greek. 'A gun is to be learned and trusted – even loved. Perhaps for a very long time. You don't just fancy a gun, little man. Not if it is the right gun.'

'He just said get it,' Lonely said.

'A magnum is a terrible weapon,' the Greek said. 'It's in the way it's made. Tremendous muzzle velocity. With a magnum bullet one can pierce a quarter inch of mild steel. Can you imagine what effect that would have on a human body? Your body, say?' The thought seemed to please him. He poured himself more wine.

'I will get you a Noguchi magnum,' he said.

'And a hundred rounds of ammo?'

'That also. Pick it up from Arthur. He will be in the Star public house. You know it?' Lonely nodded. 'Six o'clock this evening.'

'Thanks,' said Lonely. 'Thanks very much.'

'Come here,' said the Greek, and reluctantly Lonely shuffled to the kitchen table.

'This friend of yours,' said the Greek. 'Is he any good?'

'Yes,' said Lonely. 'He is. Very good.'

There was defiance in his voice, and the Greek was on to it at once.

'You have confidence in him – that he can protect you.'

'Yes,' Lonely said. 'I do.'

'Then he is not afraid to use this little thing I am getting for him?'

'I'm sorry,' Lonely said. 'I'm not at liberty to say.'

The Greek moved with a speed that was terrifying. At one moment he had been lounging in his chair, his hand cupped round the bowl of his glass, swirling the wine, the next he was on his feet, a steak-knife in his hand, the point an inch away from Lonely's throat. The hand was perfectly steady.

'But I would like to know,' the Greek said.

Lonely tried again to say 'I'm sorry', but the words wouldn't come. His entire being was aware only of the knife's needle point. Somewhere he found the strength to shake his head.

'But this is very interesting indeed,' said the Greek. 'You are even more afraid of him than you are of me.' The knife moved from Lonely's throat, and once more the Greek lounged in his chair.

'One hundred pounds, please.'

Lonely took out the bundle of fivers and counted them out, slowly.

'Six o'clock at the Star,' the Greek said again. 'Arthur will give you your goods – and your commission. All right?'

'Fine,' said Lonely. His voice was a croak.

The Greek reached out an arm, picked up an aerosol spray and sprayed the banknotes with it.

'How dreadfully you smell,' he said.

'I can't help it. I'm nervous,' Lonely said.

'Obviously,' said the Greek. Then he sprayed Lonely too.

Libraries were among Callan's favourite places. He liked the quiet, the insistence on No Smoking, the reverence bestowed on objects both inanimate and expensive by the cheap, animate misfits who treated the reference room like a vast, corporate womb. Best of all he liked just sitting with a pad and pencil beside him, copying out notes on Badajoz, or Vimeiro, or Grant's Wilderness Campaign in the American Civil War: hour after hour of research; scholarly, meticulous – and utterly useless. But today was different. Today he didn't have hours and hours: just thirty-five minutes of his lunch-hour, and Waterman at the end of it, waiting with a stop-watch. And today it wasn't the Peninsular he was researching, or Virginia. Today it was Callan's own personal and very private war: sitrep on Schneider. He turned over the pile of gazetteers and trade directories, the pages flicking faster as the minutes receded, and at last he found what he wanted: Noguchi (Yokohama) Ltd. All kinds of small arms. Specialists in recoilless rifles, light machine guns, magnum rifles and revolvers. Sole European Agents: Georges Thiers et Cie, 56, rue des Benedictines, Monte Carlo, Monaco. Rudolf Schneider (Imports and Export) Ltd. didn't even get a mention. Callan didn't even bother to write it down.

He was conscious of a faint movement behind him, and then Hunter's voice, low-pitched yet penetrating, like an archdeacon's in a cathedral:

'Callan, Callan,' Hunter said. 'What possible *use* is all this?'

Callan swivelled round in his chair. He had never known that Hunter could move so quietly. He must have been taking lessons.

'Get off my back,' he said. 'Just get off my back. Is that too much to ask?'

His voice was not angry, but he'd made no effort to lower it. All over the room the misfits looked up, greedy for excitement. This might well build up to a punch-up, perhaps with homosexual overtones. Only one ancient wreck permitted himself a 'Ssh!' and the rest hated him for it, fleetingly.

'I'll give you a lift,' said Hunter, and added before Callan could speak: 'I won't talk in front of your fan club.'

Callan pocketed his pad and pencil and left, and the misfits sighed. Not all of it was regret. There hadn't been much, but they'd had something. A rich world (Hunter's suit that morning was Savile Row) and a violent one. The hint of these things was enough: if they'd wanted reality they wouldn't have gone to the reading-room.

That Monday Hunter was using the Bentley; elderly, vast and prohibitive to run. Part office, part tank, part mobile prison. Callan and he climbed into the passenger compartment, and Hunter pressed the switch to raise the partition between passengers and driver. It was a part of Hunter's respect for the form of things that was as natural to him as breathing. A form, and nothing more. Both of them knew that the car was bugged.

Hunter said at once, 'Please stop wasting time.'

'Is that what I'm doing?'

Hunter sighed. 'Am I to assume that you

stumbled on the name Noguchi by accident?'

'No,' said Callan. 'I thought I better do some homework on the subject.'

'Did you indeed? In the idiom of your own hobby, I'd always seen your role as one of Lord Cardigan's Light Cavalry – if you follow me.'

'Sure,' said Callan. '13th Light Dragoons, 17th Lancers, 11th Hussars, 4th Light Dragoons, 8th Hussars.'

'Dashing, heroic and gorgeous,' said Hunter. 'And without a strategic thought in their heads.'

'Theirs not to reason why,' said Callan.

'Exactly,' said Hunter.

'You *do* recall the next line?'

'As I remember, they were offered a choice.'

'Yeah,' Callan said. 'Theirs but to do or die. About two hundred of them did, and about five hundred died. I don't like the odds, Hunter. I'd sooner have a few tactical thoughts.'

'I was thinking of ideal conditions of course,' said Hunter. 'And your conditions are pretty well ideal at the moment.'

'I told you,' Callan said. 'So long as the bogeys are on to him, I won't touch it.'

'The police were taken off him on Friday.

Surely I mentioned it?'

'I was waiting for you to tell me.'

'I've now done so. There's no other impediment is there?'

'A gun,' said Callan.

'I gave you money. Surely you can get one soon.'

'Tonight maybe. But I need a bit of time.'

'I'm afraid I have very little to spare.'

Callan turned to him, trying to read something, anything, in that well-bred poker face.

'What's he done, Hunter?' he asked.

'That's still not your concern. I take it you still want to come back to me?'

Reluctantly, hating himself, Callan said 'Yes.'

'Then you must meet my requirements. Kill him because I tell you to – no other reason. And do it now.'

'Not now,' said Callan. When I get that gun I've got to learn to use it right.'

'I'm not suggesting you fight a duel, Callan. A murder will be quite acceptable.'

'Yeah,' said Callan. 'Maybe. The trouble is Schneider doesn't know your rules. From what I've seen of him he carries a gun himself – and he's the boy who'd know how to use it. I don't mind doing, Hunter. But dying's out.'

'A week,' said Hunter. 'I can give you one week.'

'You're too good to me,' said Callan. 'I'll need every minute.'

They rode in silence until the car pulled up outside Callan's office block. Characteristically, Hunter hadn't asked him where he wanted to go.

'A week,' Hunter said again. 'After that I very much regret I shall have to make other arrangements.'

'For me too?'

'Your case will come up for reassessment. Inevitably. Don't scowl at me, Callan. I don't make the rules, you know that.'

'All you do is enforce them,' said Callan.

'Exactly.'

The car whispered away, and Callan climbed up the stairs, noting their grime, the feel of grit under the shoes, and contrasting them, the whole building, with the Bentley's weathered elegance. Waterman was waiting for him in his office, an excited, suspicious Waterman, and there was another contrast – Hunter and Waterman. About all they had in common was that he worked for both of them. Ostentatiously he looked at his watch. He was three minutes early.

'I saw you,' said Waterman. This made no sense at all.

'You're seeing me now,' said Callan.

Waterman was impatient. 'I saw you get here,' he said. 'Just now. In that Rolls-Royce.'

Callan said, 'Actually, it was a Bentley.' He tried to speak like Toby Meres.

'Oh, pardon my ignorance I'm sure,' said Waterman.

Callan said, 'You're welcome,' and went to his desk, began to sort out the pile of bills and invoices Waterman had shovelled on to it. It was like trying to empty an ocean with a jam jar. 'And what the hell were you doing riding in a Bentley?'

'Coming to work,' said Callan.

'And who do you know has a Bentley?'

'This bloke who picked me up.'

'Why would a bloke in a Bentley do that?'

'Maybe he fancied me,' said Callan. Waterman snorted. 'Look – it was my old CO. He recognized me and gave me a lift.'

'What for?'

'To ask how I was getting on.'

Waterman's face darkened at once. 'What did you tell him?' he asked.

'What do you think? I told him I'd just made my first million.'

Waterman still looked suspicious. 'He didn't want you to go to work for him, did he?'

Reluctantly, Callan lied.

'No,' he said.

But Waterman was still unhappy. 'I don't get it,' he said. 'You. In a Bentley.'

He went into his own office to brood.

As he worked at his figures, Callan found he didn't mind the scorn in Waterman's voice. It had been the amazement that had bothered him. He looked down at his suit, glazed by wear, the shoes, polished to a high gloss, but cracked and worn. He needed a hair-cut, and his tie was one of three, all of them old. Maybe Waterman was right to be amazed that he'd ridden in a Bentley. He looked as if he could just about afford to ride in a bus. He began to think about the Noguchi magnum 38. On a conscious level at least there seemed no connection between the gun and his poverty.

CHAPTER EIGHT

When Lonely came that night he could see at once that Callan was miserable. Tact, mate, Lonely thought. Keep it light. You don't want to upset Mr. Callan.

'I got it, Mr. Callan,' he said. 'Exactly the one you ordered.'

He said nothing about meeting Arthur in the Star, or the way Arthur made him nervous (Arthur was a heavy) or the nerve-wracking ride across London, the Noguchi in a plastic shopping bag, hidden under a mound of Brussels sprouts.

'Good lad,' said Callan. 'Let's have a look.'

Lonely burrowed cautiously into the bag, came up with a parcel, and Callan snatched it from him, scattering the wrapping paper. Like a junkie with a fix, thought Lonely, and didn't like it all. He watched, his face guarded, as Callan broke the gun, loaded it from the box of shells, snapped it together. At once he looked better.

'You know what a magnum revolver could do?' Callan asked.

'This geezer said it would go through steel-plate. Sounded barmy to me.'

'Not barmy at all,' said Callan, then: 'Which geezer?' he asked.

'Me supplier,' said Lonely, and Callan nodded. Between them there was an unspoken agreement that Lonely shouldn't mention names.

'A bloke once shot a bear with one of these,' said Callan. 'Put a bullet right through its head.'

Despite himself, Lonely said, 'You ain't going to shoot no bears, Mr. Callan.'

Callan said, 'Never mind what I'm going to shoot,' but he still looked happy. Lonely felt the fear rising in him – for once a fear for other people – and Callan sniffed.

'You still didn't buy that soap,' he said.

'You use that thing and it's life,' said Lonely.

'If they catch me. Anyway, I wouldn't tell them where I got it.'

'I wasn't thinking of that,' said Lonely. Callan looked at him, and saw that it was true.

'I think we better have a drink, old son,' he said.

The whisky came out then – what was left of it – and Callan poured two drinks.

'Here's to the Alma Mater,' he said.

'Pardon, Mr. Callan?'

'Wormwood Scrubs.' He raised his glass, and Lonely followed.

'Absent friends,' he said.

Maybe it was the whisky that gave him courage, and the heightened perception to see that Callan's room, for all its obsessive cleanliness, was no better than his own. He took another drink and watched as Callan stuck the gun into the waistband of his trousers, a reflex action, natural and sure. He could pull it out and shoot you just as easy, Lonely thought.

'What you thinking about?' asked Callan.

And that was where the courage came in.

'This gaff,' said Lonely. 'That job you pulled – the one you got done for – you shouldn't be living in a gaff like this. And anyway–' He broke off then, terrified he'd go too far.

'Go on, son,' said Callan. The voice was gentle – not like Arthur, who bullied all the time and didn't even notice he was bullying any more – more like the Greek come to think of it. Gentle because the Greek didn't have to shout: he knew you'd obey him whatever happened.

'The first time I got you a shooter I had to advance you the money. I reckon you're broke, Mr. Callan. That's why you need the gun.'

'Drink your nice whisky,' said Callan, 'and stop worrying.'

Lonely gulped at his drink, then choked. 'It's only I was thinking – I got a bit put by – if you need it like. To tide you over.'

'Thanks anyway,' said Callan, 'but I'll get my own.'

'I keep thinking of the risk,' Lonely said.

'You've never seen me use this thing. I'm good, believe me I'm good,' said Callan. And as he spoke his hand had clawed down to his waistband and came up again, the Noguchi in it, pointed unwavering at a spot above Lonely's head, while the whisky slopped in his glass, though not a drop was spilled. Callan's right hand moved again, and the gun was back at his waist. He was even faster than the Greek.

'Worry about the other feller,' said Callan.

Lonely tried once more. 'I got a ten quid introduction fee for the gun,' he said, and produced two crumpled fivers. 'I don't reckon it's right to take money off you.' He would have put them on the table then, but Callan shook his head.

'Halvers then?'

'No,' said Callan. 'You keep it, mate. Now

I've got the equipment, I'm going to be rich. When your birthday comes round I'm going to buy you a Turkish bath – all to yourself.'

When Lonely had gone, Callan thought about Schneider. He wondered if Lonely would have worried about him, too, if they'd been in the Scrubs together.

Now he'd got it, the problem was going to be to use it. He had to practise: there wasn't any other way. Draw, aim, fire, over and over, from every position, every angle, until the gun became an extension of his hand, an accusing finger you pointed at a man – and he died. He knew a place, but it was difficult to get at. To reach it he'd have to get a car. He supposed he could have asked Lonely, but any car Lonely supplied would almost certainly be nicked, and anyway the little man had done enough for him as it was. Next lunch-time he went to the post office and withdrew fifty of the eighty-three pounds that were all he had in the world. For the fifty he got an elderly Morris Minor that seemed to have been hit by everything except an eighty millimetre cannon; but its brakes were good, it had a reconditioned engine and its steering, if eccentric, was at least consistent. That evening, after work, he took it out on a trial run: across the City, up to the West End, then northwards on to the Circular Road, missing the A1 and the M1, finishing up at last in Hertfordshire, nine miles from nowhere, a decaying road that led to a deserted spinney: old trees, un-pruned raspberry bushes, nettles and couch grass, a choked stream forcing its way through it, the paths long since obliterated. Around the spinney a railway track ran in a great arc, and behind the track was a quarry. The noise was appalling: the tumbling crash of stone into metal trucks, the clattering of buffers, the banging and fussing of shunting engines. Nothing could compete against that, not even a magnum 38.

He parked the car in a lay-by, walked back down the road and ducked under a broken fence, then sprawled prone behind a clump of briar. A Triumph Vitesse went past: min-utes later a maroon Jaguar followed. They'd done a nice job: tailing in a car is never easy, but these men were experts. Soon now Hunter would know where Callan was, and get out his large-scale map of the district, and know exactly what Callan was doing... Callan walked into the spinney, cautious of the tus-socks of grass that could send him sprawling, and around him the din continued. Callan pushed on to the stream and found what he wanted, a post of hard wood, and nailed to it a noticeboard, half eaten away with rot. The almost obliterated letters appeared to be about picnicking and trespassing. The man must have been deaf, Callan thought. No mania for privacy could compete against this row.

Suddenly the gun flicked into his hand, he stood in the classic stance of the pistol shooter. As if I was in the bloody Olympics, he thought. Grow up, Callan. When are *you* going to get a chance to loose off standing like that? But it was a new gun, its secrets still unlearned. Best to treat it nicely, at least to start with.

He fired, slow and even, squeezing the trigger the way the textbooks said you should in a steady rhythm of fire, aiming at the post at a point below the notice-board. A nice gun, he thought. Pulls a bit to the left, but not much. Trigger action lighter than the Smith and Wesson: noise about the same. The Japs have come on a bit. Cameras ... motor-bikes ... super tankers ... and guns... Suddenly the post snapped in two, the notice-board fell to the ground. Callan walked up and looked at the damage, and spoke aloud.

'Jesus,' he said.

Each magnum bullet had gone straight through the post, and the post was weathered wood, six inches in section, then embedded itself in a beech tree beyond, to a depth of a foot at least. Callan had read about magnums, and accepted in his mind the things they could do, but to see the visual evidence like this was incredible – even horrifying. With this gun he could shoot through an oak door, kill the man behind it, and the man behind *him*. The muzzle velocity of the bullet, as it left the barrel, was unbelievable. But the gun had its limitations too. It was a marksman's weapon, not a stopper. To be sure of stopping a man you needed a slower, heavier bullet, 45 calibre say. A slug like that would knock you down and stay inside you no matter where it hit: but a 38 magnum bullet would hit you and keep on going till it came out the other side, the exit hole no bigger than the entry hole, and unless you got a vital place a determined man with the adrenalin really flowing would still keep on coming at you. Callan remembered reading about a determined man who'd had four magnum bullets go through him and still managed to knife the bloke who'd fired them. There weren't all that many vital places either: brain shots and heart shots, or the knee cap if you didn't want the bloke to die. He took a piece of chalk from his pocket and drew two shapes on a beech tree, the size of Schneider's forehead and heart. At the last moment he added a knee-cap too. After that it was draw, aim, fire, draw, aim, fire, sitting, standing, lying, kneeling, using every possible position, as the dusk drew in and the light got worse. He went on until the last possible minute: conditions for his kind of killing were always less than ideal. When he stopped at last he'd fired thirty rounds, and Schneider had been killed twenty-one times, ten through the head, eleven through the heart, and had seven bullets in his knee-cap.

I've still got it, Callan thought. I could go up to Hampstead and shoot him dead this minute. But Hunter had given him a week, and he knew he'd use it. In his heart he knew he wasn't ready to kill again. Not yet.

Meres said, 'Lonely went to Knightsbridge, sir, I had to put three people on to him – and even then they couldn't get too close. He's a cautious little man. And very smelly.'

Hunter looked up. 'You went yourself?'

'I thought I'd better take a look at him,' said Meres. Hunter nodded: the nod told Meres nothing. 'He disappeared down a mews. He was carrying one of those plastic bags with a picture of Lord Kitchener on it.'

'Picture of whom?'

'Lord Kitchener, sir.' Meres enjoyed the puzzlement in Hunter's eyes. 'It's what is called trendy.'

'But why Kitchener?' Hunter asked.

'People find him amusing, sir.'

'*Amusing?*' Hunter said. 'My uncle was on his staff. He didn't find him amusing.' He blinked, became impassive again. 'Go on.'

'When he came out he had the gun in it.'

'D'you know where he got it?'

'No, sir.'

'Your police friends know of anyone round there?'

'I'm afraid not. I thought it unwise to follow him too closely sir.'

'Quite right,' Hunter said. 'We know he's got it, we know he's practising with it – all we need to know now is will he use it.' He yawned and stretched in his chair. 'Better keep up your target practice, Toby.'

'I will, sir,' said Meres. He found it impossible to keep the look of eagerness from his face.

'I'll bid you goodnight then,' said Hunter.

'Goodnight, sir.'

Meres left, and Hunter thought about him;

his mind concentrated solely on Meres for two minutes. So far, Meres was useful. Drove his men hard, drove himself hard. Cold nerve, excellent shot, no qualms about killing – on the contrary. Meres liked killing. Needed it in fact. The way some people need drugs. And like a drug addict's, Meres' needs were cumulative. One day Meres would be hard to restrain: eventually restraint would be impossible. When that day came, dear Toby too would have to be eliminated. Hunter hoped it wouldn't be for a long time: killers were very difficult to replace. Callan was an excellent example. He thought of Schneider then, clearing his mind of every other consideration. There'd been a signal from Kuala Lumpur that morning. The Indonesians had started demonstrations again: boy fanatics had taken all sorts of vows to make Borneo part of the Indonesian republic. Some of them even vowed chastity, until Merdeka dawned. Merdeka – freedom. Maybe the people of Borneo thought they were free already, but that wouldn't stop the Indonesians. They'd go on till Borneo got the kind of freedom Indonesia wanted it to have. That meant landing trigger-happy idiots who called themselves commandos in Borneo and shooting up everything and everybody in sight. Not troops, though. That would be going too far. And not using standard army issue weapons. At the United Nations even the Afro-Asian bloc would find that a little hard to swallow. No. They would go to the arms smugglers, and the arms smugglers would go to the nearest wholesaler, which was the firm called Noguchi, of Yokohama. Unless of course something happened to persuade the arms dealers that trading with Indonesia, though lucrative, was unwise. If one of them were to die, say – Hunter looked at his calendar. It would be best if Schneider were dead by Friday. It would be convenient, too. He'd been invited to a dinner and bridge on Saturday, and he was quite sure he would win.

Next day was an easy one for Callan. The accounts were almost up to date, and Waterman left early. Once he'd gone Callan locked the office door and opened up the battered leather case that he'd carried to the City every morning, the case that contained his sandwiches, his flask of coffee, and whatever military history he read in his lunchhour, and took out the Noguchi, stuck it in his waistband, aimed it, squeezed the trigger on the empty barrel, did it over and over,

136

then rested, massaged his fingers, wrist and biceps, repeated the process, feeling the suppleness flow back to his hand and arm, knowing himself not ready yet, but moving closer. The Callan he'd thought was dead had only slept, after all, and now his sleep was uneasy.

At five o'clock he thought of leaving, but realized in time that Waterman would have thought of it too, and sure enough Waterman called him at twenty-five past – five minutes before he was due to leave. He sounded disappointed when Callan answered, and kept him talking till twenty to six. When Callan left at last, he paused outside Schneider's door. Schneider was talking.

'My darling,' he was saying, 'Why do you worry so much? Worry will make you go thin. How can I hold you as I like if you lose weight?'

There was a silence, then Schneider spoke again. 'Darling, believe me,' he said, 'it will be all right. No. Much more than all right. It will be beautiful.'

Another silence, and then Schneider said something in a language Callan couldn't recognize, and there was the sound of a telephone put back on the hook. Callan moved off quickly. On the way out he passed

Schneider's chauffeur, loping up the stairs three at a time. He was carrying a telegram form, and he looked as if Mafeking had just been relieved and he was the first to know about it. Callan went down to the Morris Minor, and set off for Hertfordshire again. As he drove he thought about Schneider. He'd got good news, that was obvious, and good news for him meant bad news for Hunter (if he found out about it – and what had ever happened that bastard hadn't found out?) and bad news for Hunter meant bad news for Schneider. Or rather, Callan corrected himself, bad news for Schneider's nearest and dearest. And that brought him to the bird. It came as no surprise to Callan that Schneider had a bird, and Callan was willing to bet she'd be a knockout. Schneider might be pushing fifty, but he was in damn good nick, and good-looking too, in a hard sort of way. The bird he got would have no complaints about her sex life. And there'd be other things too: the food, the wine, the presents. Schneider wouldn't stint. He was everything a bird dreams about. Callan wondered if she'd weep for him.

A bird had wept for Callan once: wept out loud in court when the judge put him down for two years. A bird called Shirley. She'd been a typist. Blonde. Blue eyes. A little bird. He'd loved the way she had to tilt her head back to look at him, as well as her neat figure, the softness of her mouth. She hadn't known much in bed, not at first, but he'd taught her, and she'd been dead keen to learn. He'd spent money on her too willingly, because she made him so happy. Maybe he'd done that safe partly for her. Not that he blamed her: she'd never had the remotest idea... When she'd written to him at the Scrubs she said she'd wait for him. For ever and ever if need be. He'd seen her once, when he'd come out. Pushing a pram, and another kid on the way. The blonde hair had gone back to mouse colour, and her eyes weren't the blue he remembered. She'd walked straight past him.

When he reached the spinney the memory of Shirley was still with him: it had made him randy – and that wasn't on, not when he'd come out to practise. He lay in the same cover as before, waiting for the cars that trailed him, and continued to lie still after they had passed, breathing slowly, evenly, till the heat died in him. He found another tree, and drew his targets again, then began firing, snap shots, to the background of the clattering trucks. It was on the seventeenth shot that the memory hit him, and with it a picture: a brothel in Singapore, and himself with a Malay girl on his knees, feeding him Tiger beer. In the background two Chinese whores were quarrelling, and the sounds they made had been like the sounds Schneider had made on the telephone. It looked as if Schneider had a Chinese bird. Callan looked at the target, alarmed at his loss of concentration, but it was all right. Memories or no memories, Schneider would still have been dead.

Hunter had him followed on the Wednesday too, but on Thursday they seemed to think he was all right. There was just one car, and it left him at the North Circular. That was a break he needed, and he didn't waste it, but he went first to the spinney even so, and fired off ten rounds rapid, which left him with thirty, then drove to Hampstead, and the Vale of Health. The car was wrong for the area, and Callan knew it, parked, and walked to Schneider's house, carrying the attaché case; the little insurance agent chancing his luck in the haunts of the wealthy in the hope of a thirty-quid commission, and knowing damn well he wouldn't get it. Callan thought of Bethany, and his terrible Health Food samples.

Schneider's house wasn't enormous, but even millionaires didn't run to enormous houses in the Vale of Health, where a pound note bought approximately the amount of ground it could cover. But there was a garden, and not just a patch of lawn, and the house itself, unashamedly early Victorian, was a house, and not just a collection of hutches. Callan walked quickly past it to the end of the road, where there was a telephone box. He went inside, picked up the receiver and began a long conversation with one of the screws who'd done him over in the Scrubs, analysing his shortcomings in pitiless detail, and all the time watching Schneider's house. He could afford to wait ten minutes, just in case. And luck was with him. After three minutes Schneider and a girl came out. The girl wore expensive tweeds and hand-lasted brogues and would have looked as debby as hell, if she hadn't been Chinese. They set off towards the heath, and shortly afterwards the chauffeur came out too, walking briskly. Callan left the phone box and followed, keeping his distance, until the chauffeur turned into a pub. Any other ser-vants? Callan wondered. Cook? Housekeeper maybe? Anyway it was worth a try.

He went back to Schneider's house and

opened the gate. No dog in the garden. Mr. Schneider, you're a trusting soul, thought Callan, and walked up the path, rang the bell once, then again. No answer. Too trusting, Callan thought, and took out the key he had copied, opened the front door and went inside. The hallway was warm, its floor covered with a carpet of Chinese silk. Carefully, Callan wiped his feet on the doormat then looked around for the meter. It was in a far corner of the room, and Callan remembered, just in time, not to rush at it. Instead, he pulled on a pair of rubber gloves and stood stock still, examining the room with infinite patience until he spotted it: a photoelectric cell smack in front of the meter, two feet from the floor. He got down on his back and wriggled beneath it, then reached up and switched off the power supply. That made life easier. He looked round quickly. Downstairs was a kitchen, dining-room, living-room and study: and in the study was the safe. All the same – better to check upstairs too. Upstairs were five bedrooms – four of them unused, the fifth the perfect setting for a magnificent double-bed (Enjoy it Schneider. You don't have much time) and a bathroom that also looked as if it might be fun. But where did the chauffeur sleep? Over the garage? Callan went downstairs again and into the study.

He opened his case and knelt before the safe. A pre-war job, a Mason and Jones. The one they called the 'Thiefproof'. A laugh that was. A key safe with a gimmick; that's all it was. So long as you used the right key and turned it the right way it opened as easy as your back door. You use the wrong key, or turn the right key the wrong way and the lock jammed. You were knackered. And as only you (the Thiefproof's proud owner) knew the right way to turn the key, the family tiara was safe from the villains, property stayed sacred and law and order triumphed once more. Except, thought Callan, that it didn't work like that. Nowadays you didn't probe locks with a bloody great lump of steel – not these locks anyway – you used fine wire and probed and teased till it showed you the shape of the key, and when you had that you took out a Mason and Jones key blank which, being a careful worker, you'd added to your collection, and filed it to the shape the wire had shown you. And when that was done, if you'd been apprentice of the year at Bartram's all you had to do was look at the key and you knew which way it would turn. Ten minutes for the whole job, and up yours Mason and Jones.

The whole thing's too bloody easy, thought Callan. You're a very careless man, Mr. Schneider. And untidy too. Look at the mess in your office. Waterman would fire you in a week. Break your heart that would, Schneider old love. Now then. He inserted the key and turned it the only possible way: one right, two left, four right. It didn't come willingly, but it came, and Callan eased it open – careful, not too far – switched on a pencil torch and squinted inside.

'Yeah,' he said to himself. 'I thought so. Nobody's that careless, are they, Mr. Schneider?' Wired to the inside of the safe was another burglar alarm, and this one worked off a bloody great battery. Gently, hands light as butterflies, Callan disconnected it and pulled the safe door open. The top three shelves were empty, but the fourth one seemed at first glance to be solid with money. Pound notes, fivers, Swiss francs, dollars. Not in a mess either, but stacked according to nationality in neat blocks of a hundred. He explored further, behind the bundles of money, and came out with a handful of invoices, clipped together, a neat stack, in chronological order. All were for goods supplied by Noguchi: rifles, pistols, sub-machine guns, grenades. As he put them back, his fingers touched more papers. He coaxed them out, and they were newspaper clippings. Every one told the same story: trouble in Malaysia, or Borneo; Indonesian invaders in running battles with HM Forces; the names, sometimes the faces, of the British dead. Callan sighed aloud. Congratulations, old man, he thought. You're doing a marvellous job. I like you – I even respect you, I really do– And I'm going to have to kill you.

He shut up the safe then, first re-connecting the burglar alarm. His movements were brisk and assured, yet cautious too; the movements of a professional doing a somewhat dangerous job, and giving the danger its due deference. He put his tools away then, and picked up the attaché case. It would have to be the front door again. The back door was bolted, and there wasn't time to fiddle the bolt. But before he left he took another look in the living-room. It was dominated by a huge table, and on it a battle was laid out, miniature soldiers in khaki and field grey, armed with rifles, bayonets and grenades, trench-mortars and machine guns, and field guns up in support. First World War stuff, the Battle of Mons maybe. Too recent and too unimaginative for Callan's taste. Beside the table was a chest made of teak. Callan lifted its lid and inside, as he suspected, it was divided into compartments lined with velvet. Each compartment containing model soldiers, beautifully made, correct to the last detail. Callan picked out a grey clad horseman, one of Jeb Stuart's men, in the Army of the Confederacy. That had really been a war. He put it back and replaced the lid on the chest. As he prepared to leave, he looked again at the Battle of Mons, his eye caught and held by a German captain rallying his men, waving a Luger pistol.

'You were right, Schneider old love,' said Callan. 'You should have stuck to playing soldiers.'

He went out by the front door, after he had switched on the meter, and nobody bothered, nobody even looked. Sixteen minutes for the whole job. He could have been walking out with fifty thousand quid, and Lonely could have got him a passport in three hours. With fifty thousand quid he could have lain for a year in the sun, then bought himself a nice little bar somewhere and lived slow and easy for the rest of his life. And yet the idea hadn't even occurred to him till after he'd left the place. But then he wasn't interested in thieving.

CHAPTER NINE

He went back to the Morris Minor. It was no surprise at all to see Meres waiting beside it. In this business people were always bobbing up unannounced. It was an occupational hazard, like being followed, or tortured – or shot. You learned to live with it. Callan walked up to Meres and let his face show nothing at all. Meres hadn't surprised him, but he had annoyed him, and the annoyance was an irrelevance, or worse, a distraction. He detested Meres, and the detestation like any other emotion, had to be controlled or it slowed you up.

'What a terrible motor car,' said Meres.

There was nothing in that for Callan. He let it pass.

'I'm afraid I'm going to have to ride in it,' Meres continued. 'Too ghastly.'

'Who says you're going to have to ride in it?'

'Charlie. He wants to see you. Now. This very minute.'

'In his office?'

'Where else?'

Callan made no answer, unlocked the doors, and Meres settled gingerly in the front passenger seat, like a new yogi on his first bed of nails, thought Callan, and drove off carefully, mindful of policemen, a law-abiding citizen who wanted no trouble, not when he was carrying a kit of burglars' tools and a magnum revolver. He drove across London from North to South, from the posh end to the dead end, from riches to rags, and finished up at last in the totty school playground. And all the way Meres had nagged him about his poverty, in that play-acting pansy-clever voice of his, and all the way Callan had driven in silence. Fighting with Meres was an irrelevance. Forget it. When they got out at last Meres stretched like a cat, and Callan was aware of the tremendous force in the slender body.

'Thank goodness that's over,' said Meres. 'I'd have been more comfortable on top of the corporation dustcart.'

Callan made one concession to irrelevance.

'What's the matter, Toby?' he asked. 'Won't Hunter let you kill anybody?'

The threat came at once, and Callan was ready for it, hands loose, body relaxed, waiting for Meres to strike, and for a second

Meres almost did let go, right there under Hunter's eyes. Callan could see the enormous effort of will he had to exert to bring himself back from the madness, an exertion that left him shaking. At last, somehow, he managed a laugh.

'Well well,' said Meres. 'I'd forgotten what a bitch you can be when you try.'

Callan went back to silence.

This time when they rang the bell Vic made no move to search him, or to examine the contents of his case. All he said was, 'Charlie says wait in the gallery,' and to the gallery they went. He came down to them almost at once, not hurrying; but not dawdling either. Hunter rarely played the superior keeping the minion in his place game, and when he did it always had a purpose. On the other hand he didn't believe in hurrying either. Hurrying made for carelessness.

'Wotcher, Charlie,' said Callan.

Hunter ignored him and turned to Meres.

'Was he at Schneider's?' he asked.

'Yes, sir,' said Meres.

'Thank you, Toby. I needn't keep you,' Hunter said, then as Meres turned to go – 'No. That's not quite true I'm afraid. I was watching you. On the television, you know. It was my impression that at one moment

149

you were about to strike Callan.'

Meres was silent.

'Toby, that sentence, though couched in the form of a statement, was in effect a question.'

'I wanted to hit him, yes, sir. But I didn't,' Meres said at last.

'I think you were wise,' said Hunter, and added, 'that really is all. For now.'

Meres left.

'You think I would have clobbered him?' Callan asked.

'I think you would have tried – if he'd attacked you first. You have more cunning than Toby. It's more than possible that you would have won. Though Toby *is* very good, on occasion extremely good. But you mustn't fight till the Schneider affair is over. I hope that's clear?' Callan nodded. 'After that you can put him in the hospital, if it makes you feel any better. Provided of course you don't injure him too severely.'

He *must* be in a hurry, thought Callan. He's never tried the indulgent father bit before.

'Why did you go to Schneider's house?' asked Hunter.

'How did you know I'd go there?'

'I didn't. Though I was aware that you

150

might. That's why I didn't have you tailed this evening.'

'And sent Toby to meet me?'

'Precisely. He would have been useful, too, if Schneider and the girl or the chauffeur had got back too early.'

'He reported in then, did he?' Callan asked.

'Of course.'

'You know why I went to Schneider's house, Hunter,' Callan said.

'To find out what he'd done. Did you find out?'

'Yes,' said Callan.

'Against my express orders.'

'I'm not a Toby Meres,' said Callan. 'I have to know why.'

'And now you do know why?'

'Yes,' said Callan. 'He's an arms smuggler. He's got a lot of our blokes killed.'

'Does that make it ethical enough for you?' Hunter asked.

'No. But it makes it necessary,' said Callan.

'Good. Do you have that Noguchi revolver with you? If so, I should like to see you use it. On Prendergast.'

Prendergast was a target dummy with a sorbo rubber head of simpering prettiness. From time to time the heads had to be replaced, but it made no difference; they were all the same.

Callan put ten bullets into Prendergast, from a variety of positions and in bad light. Eight of them would have been fatal wounds, and Prendergast needed a new head.

'I think you're ready,' Hunter said.

'So do I,' said Callan.

'In that case I should like you to kill Schneider tomorrow. I know you hate to be rushed, Callan, but the matter is extremely urgent.'

'Does it matter where I do it?'

'Not in the least,' said Hunter.

'It better be his house then. Attempted burglary – you know. Plucky householder intervenes – the burglar panics. Suddenly a shot rings out–' And then he stopped.

'It can't, can it?' said Hunter. 'There's the girl to consider.'

'I've considered her,' Callan said. 'And the chauffeur. It isn't that.'

'What then?'

'That safe's full of loot. And Noguchi in-voices. And newspaper clippings. Clippings about the blokes who got killed. I'll have to get rid of them, won't I?'

'No,' said Hunter.

'But the rozzers'll see them. They'll know that's why he was killed.'

'Perhaps the girl will destroy them before the police arrive – but I hope not. If she does I'll have to plant others in Schneider's office. Perhaps you'd better steal some of them. I want Schneider's business known, Callan.'

'But why?'

'You don't imagine he's the only one, do you? If he were there'd be no point in killing him. A simple warning might do it. There are lots of others. And Indonesia is a very hungry market for arms. If the arms dealers know that someone is prepared to kill them – Indonesia will go on being hungry.'

'Always provided you're right,' Callan said.

'If I'm wrong, you can kill the next one for me – provided you get this one right.'

'You'll take me back then?'

'There is a possibility,' said Hunter. 'That's all I'm prepared to say at the moment.'

He turned away then, and looked at Prendergast. The interview was almost over.

'I'll leave you to work out the details,' he said. 'God knows you've had enough experience.' Callan winced. 'A nice simple job, Callan. That's all I want. That – and three or four invoices and clippings. Oh – and the money. Such useful stuff – and we never have

enough. You can have ten per cent. All right?'
Callan nodded. 'I'll bid you goodnight then,'
said Hunter, 'Don't call again until you have
good news.'

Parking the car was always a problem in
Duke William Street, but he found a place at
last, and locked it carefully. Nobody but a
nut would pinch a wreck like that, but Duke
William Street had more than enough nuts
to go round, and he'd need that car tomorrow. Five thousand quid, he thought. He'd
be able to buy something a bit better once
he'd got his paws on that. Find a decent flat:
buy more soldiers, too. Five thousand quid
was a hell of a lot if you didn't have to pay
tax on it. Suddenly Callan realized that he
didn't want a ha'penny of it. Didn't even
want to steal it for Hunter. He's turning me
into a bleeding Mafioso. Not even that.
Murder Incorporated.

He walked along the street and passed a
bunch of youngsters in Afghan coats, long
hair, straggling beards. One of them carried a
transistor radio, its pop music dominating
the street noises: guitars twanging like the
ganglia of giants, drum beat like a boot in the
crutch, the hermaphrodite voice screaming
over and over: It's lurv, it's lurv, it's lurv. But

154

how could it be if you're a hermaphrodite? Callan wondered... Flower children. Junior gurus. Like I don't make the scene man. Like I'm thirty-four years old and that's only seventeen years away from them, and for all the communication we've got they might as well be Martians. Maybe Hunter's having a rundown on them, he thought. Just in case he finds he needs a hippy killer.

They split apart suddenly, and let him through. Beside them a Mercedes 600 waited at the kerb, and the flower kids looked at it as though it were scrap-iron. That was a strength they had, and Callan coveted it. Money didn't move them. They didn't need it. Money to them simply meant possessions, gadgets, and to gadgets they were immune. They'd seen too many. He carried on into Stanmore House and began to climb the stairs. The stairs had rubber treads and a liberal allowance of grit. Callan detested them. In his day-dreams sometimes he commandeered a fire-engine and used it to hose down those stairs, then covered them with wall to wall carpeting, and had it sprayed with French perfume. Then he commandeered a petrol tanker and set fire to Stanmore House.

There was a bloke coming down the stairs:

a big bloke, built like a wrestler. Only wrestlers didn't usually wear single-breasted dark blue business suits and bowler hats. Probably a bailiff, Callan thought. Or a process server. He kept on going and the big bloke moved aside to let him pass, then looked over his shoulder as Callan took out his key and went to the door. The big bloke moved nice and quiet, and Callan had no chance at all. One moment he had his key in the lock, and was preparing to worry the night away, going over in his mind his plans for Schneider, the next a thick arm encircled his neck, squeezed with a scientifically controlled force, and Callan was lifted bodily round on the stairhead as a hand explored him for weapons.

'There's a feller downstairs wants a word with you,' said Arthur. 'It'll be nice if you come down quiet.' The grip on his throat tightened momentarily, and Callan felt as if his eyes were ballooning in their sockets, then the pressure relaxed.

'What d'you say?' the big bloke said.

There was no point in fighting: the big bloke had all the advantages. There was no point in losing contact either. The big bloke was an unknown, and so was the feller downstairs. It was necessary to know who they were; what they were doing.

'What the hell is this all about?' said Callan. It was the right question, but he sounded querulous and unsure of himself, a man trying to bluff. It wasn't acting: that was the way he felt.

'You want me to squeeze you again?' the big bloke asked.

'No, darling. I couldn't take any more to-night,' Callan whispered.

'Then walk ahead of me down the stairs. Try anything and I'll belt you.'

Callan did as he was ordered. When they reached the bottom of the stairs the big bloke's arm reached out, in what looked like a brotherly embrace. To anyone watching the big bloke was helping a drunken friend. Only Callan knew that he had fingers like rivets and that two of them were pressing on the nerve under Callan's jaw. If he tried to yell, Callan knew exactly what would happen. It would not be pleasant.

As they appeared in the doorway, the Mercedes moved out, then stopped, and its door swung open. The flower children watched, unimpressed. Drunks were no novelty in their lives, and usually they were a drag any-way. Callan reached the car and the big bloke boosted him neatly into the seat next to the driver, then got in himself, and again encircled Callan in his arm; his fingers found the nerve centre. Callan gasped and went limp, and the big bloke detached the leather case from Callan's hands, and laid it across his own massive knees as the car moved into the traffic.

'Very nice, Arthur,' the driver said. 'Is he unconscious?'

'No,' said Arthur. 'Just resting. Aren't you, son?'

'You keep it up and I'll be dead,' said Callan. His throat burned from the pressure of the serge clad arm, the nerve-ends Arthur had pressed jangled like guitar strings. Arthur chuckled.

'There won't be any more,' he said. 'Not if you're going to cooperate.'

'I'm co-operating now,' said Callan. 'I did what you told me, didn't I?'

He could hear the terror in his voice. Again he didn't have to act.

'Did he?' the driver asked.

'Yeah,' said Arthur. He sounded disappointed.

They drove on, skirting the park, past a big hotel lit up like an ocean liner, then vanished into a maze of back streets.

'Where you taking me?' Callan asked.

158

'Later,' the driver said.

'Look here what *is* this?' said Callan.

Again Arthur's hand engulfed Callan's neck.

'Gently, Arthur,' said the driver.

'All right,' said Callan. 'All right!'

Arthur's finger pressed quickly, a mere hint of the pain that would follow if Callan were difficult. But Callan had no intention of being difficult. There was too much to learn.

'Give him a cigarette,' the driver said.

'I don't smoke,' said Callan, and the driver scowled.

Callan thought: He didn't like that. I broke the pattern for him. He's after a two man interrogation set up. One man hurts you; the other man tries to help. More hurt: more help. First a bashing, then a cup of tea. Then another bashing. If you don't confess to the heavy to stop the pain, you spill it all to the nice guy out of gratitude. It's so old it creaks. But it usually works.

They pulled up outside a garage, the driver pressed a button on the dashboard and the garage door swung up and over. He took the car inside, pressed the button again, the door swung back into place. Arthur got out, and held the car door open.

'Out!' he said, and Callan did as he was told. The driver got out at the other side. Callan looked at him. Medium height, olive complexion, sleek as a seal, with the soulful eyes of a Neapolitan singer. Running very slightly to fat, but hard underneath it. Harder even than Arthur.

'This way,' he said, and walked across the garage. Callan followed, and Arthur brought up the rear. It was a big garage, big enough for two trucks as well as the Merc. It had work benches and an inspection pit, and behind it a windowless room with a cooker, table, chairs and a bed. The sleek man with the soulful eyes entered the room, and as Callan followed Arthur spun him round and hit him in belly. The force of the blow was as carefully controlled as the pressure of his fingers, but even so the pain scalded through Callan, his stomach heaved, and he pitched forward on to his knees. Arthur hit him across the face then, an open-handed slap that sent him sprawling.

'I told you to wait,' said the sleek man. 'This may not be necessary.' He looked down at Callan.

'Believe me, I don't want it to be necessary,' he said.

Arthur moved over to Callan.

'Get up,' he said, and Callan obeyed him, as slowly as he dared. He could not risk another blow, but he needed time to get his strength back, even to think coherently. At the moment, the only thing he knew was that his stomach ached abominably.

The sleek man said, 'All we want you to do is to answer some questions.'

'Can I sit down?' Callan asked.

'Of course.' The sleek man pushed forward a chair and Callan fell into it. The sleek man sat down then, facing Callan across the table, and Arthur stayed standing by Callan, looking like a switched-off machine. A machine for hurting people. One word, one look, would set him working again.

'Your name is Callan. David Callan.' Callan nodded. 'Where do you work, Mr. Callan?'

'Waterman's. It's a firm of wholesale grocers in the City.'

'Forgive the impertinence, Mr. Callan, but have you ever been to prison?'

'Of course not,' Callan said.

The machine came back to life. Again Arthur's hand swung, and Callan was knocked back in his chair.

'Sit up,' said Arthur, immobile again. He had hands like oak boards. Already Callan's ear was buzzing. If this went on, his ear drums would be smashed.

'If you tell the truth you won't be hurt,' the sleek man said. 'Now let us try again. Have you ever been to prison?'

'Yes,' said Callan. 'Wormwood Scrubs. I did two years for robbery. Look, mister. Please. What is this all about?'

'First the questions. They won't take long,' said the sleek man.

Callan sat up in his chair, moving to face the man across the table. That brought his right hand closer to Arthur. He was going to need all the impetus he could get if he had to hit Arthur from a sitting position. Arthur was hard all over.

'What's in that case?'

'A gun,' said Callan.

The sleek man smiled. 'Is it by any chance a Noguchi centre fire magnum revolver, 38 calibre?' he asked.

So that's who you are, thought Callan. Lonely old lad, you're slipping.

'That's right,' he said.

'Anything else?' the sleek man asked.

'Isn't that enough?'

For that Arthur put his fingers to the nerve ends in Callan's neck again.

'I'm sorry,' Callan gasped. 'It's just I don't understand what this is all about.'

'I should like to see the gun,' said the sleek man, and put the case on the table.

'It's locked,' said Callan.

'Naturally. The key please.'

Callan's hand moved to his pocket, then he got to his feet. It was the perfectly natural reaction of a man whose keys were eluding him, and he got away with it because the sleek man and Arthur thought he was well on the way to being broken. His hand went back to his pocket. For anyone Arthur's size there was only one way that would give Callan any kind of chance at all. That was atimi, the attacking blows of karate. It might also turn out to be murder, but as Hunter never tired of telling him, when you kill in defence of your country, it isn't murder. It's war.

His weight came down on his front foot, and for a split second Arthur knew what Callan was going to do. It wasn't enough. His right hand came up from his pocket in a three finger strike that stabbed exactly at a point just below the inverted V of Arthur's rib cage, the aim straightening just before the moment of contact to give extra impetus. The one blow was enough to transform Arthur from crude power to inanimate mass, but Callan had already unleashed the follow-up, a left hand chop to the side of Arthur's neck: all his strength meeting all Arthur's descending weight, holding it fractionally so that the final throat punch, a right-hander, pushed Arthur backwards over the table and on top of the sleek man, who had started to get up far too late. Sleek man, Arthur and table fell together, intermingling as they went. The sleek man wriggled like a cat, and escaped from the table, but Arthur was another matter. Arthur must have weighed eighteen stone at least, and he wasn't helping at all. Callan unlocked the case, took out the magnum and showed it to the sleek man as he emerged at last from under Arthur. The sleek man froze.

'Just like you said. A Noguchi magnum centre fire revolver, 38 calibre,' said Callan.

The sleek man said, 'I think you've killed Arthur.'

'I think so too,' said Callan. 'Take a look.'

The sleek man said something in what Callan thought was Greek, then knelt by Arthur, turned him over, felt for the heart beat, put his face close to Arthur's mouth.

'He's dead,' he said at last.

'Go ahead and cry if you want to. We British don't show our emotions so easily,' said Callan.

Cautiously the sleek man stood up, his whole body aware of the revolver.

'I'm beginning to think I made a mistake about you.'

'That's right,' said Callan. 'Have you got any whisky?'

'In the cupboard.'

'Get it,' said Callan, and the sleek man obeyed; Callan and the revolver watching his every move.

'Have one yourself,' said Callan. 'You've had a bit of a shock.'

The sleek man poured two glasses and drank his quickly, avidly. The fingers of Callan's left hand rubbed solicitously at his stomach. Arthur really had known how to hit. He drank a little Scotch.

'Friend of yours?' he asked.

'An employee,' the sleek man said.

'Just who are you?' Callan asked.

'My name's Papadopoulos. Over here I'm known as the Greek. It's easier.'

'You got me this?' The magnum moved in his hand, aimed at the bridge of Papado-poulos' nose.

'It was the one Lonely asked for,' the Greek said.

'Don't think I'm not grateful,' said Callan. 'It was a hundred quid well spent. But what the hell do you think you're playing at tonight?'

The Greek said, 'It's rather a long story.'

Callan sat down, and motioned to the other to do the same.

'You may have time,' he said. 'On the other hand you may not. Tell it as quick as you can.'

Beneath the table his legs were shaking; the inevitable reaction to what he'd done, but the hand clamped round the gun stayed steady.

'Lonely came to get a gun for you. You know that,' said the Greek, and Callan nodded. 'But after a bit I started to think – why Lonely? He's not exactly the killer type. It made me wonder about you. Who you were. What you were up to. Lonely seemed very impressed with you. Then Lonely brought the first gun back – the Smith and Wesson, and I forgot all about it – till he came back again for the Noguchi. That interested me.'

'Why?' Callan asked.

'It suggested that you'd had a job lined up and for some reason it was put off – then it was on again, and in the meantime you'd had second thoughts about the gun – you switched from an ordinary 38 to a magnum.

166

This made me think that you were either a craftsman or a damned fool – because with a magnum one must be extremely accurate. I decided to find out which. I have no time for fools, Mr. Callan.'

'Me neither,' said Callan. 'They're almost as bad as blokes that pry into other blokes' business.'

The Greek shuddered. He was doing his best to hide it, but the fear was getting to him.

'Get on with it.' Callan said.

'I had Lonely followed,' he said.

'Now that is an achievement,' Callan said.

'I know he's a cautious little man, but his psychology is very simple. Arthur handed the gun to him.' He looked quickly, unwillingly, at the body on the floor. 'I told Arthur to put a scare into him. That made Lonely nervous, and the nervousness made him careless. I had three people tailing him – two men and a woman.'

'That must have cost you,' Callan said.

'I hoped it would be worth it.'

'How?'

'If I thought you were a man who knew his business, I intended to– I considered that–'

'You were going to cut yourself in on the take.'

The Greek nodded. The way he was looking at the magnum, it seemed to fill his world.

'You done it before?' Callan asked. The Greek nodded again. 'Got any form?'

'Prison? No. Not in this country.'

'Doing all right, are you?' Callan asked. The Greek hesitated. 'Don't lie to me, son. You must be. Look at your clothes, that watch. Merc 600. Arthur. He wouldn't come cheap. You're big time.'

The Greek said, 'Very big. You better remember that.'

At once Callan's legs stopped shaking. Threats he could handle.

'Spell it out,' he said. 'Don't go coy on me.'

'I did a lot of homework on you,' the Greek said. 'You did a job all right. A big job. Solo. Arthur talked to a man who knew you in the nick. You had a bit of trouble with some men who tried to form a tobacco syndicate.'

'I handled it,' said Callan.

'So I heard. Then you got out. You "went straight", as they say. It's over ten years now. But you have an itch, Callan. A need. You are a violent man. An ambitious man. In the last analysis, you are a very dangerous man. And your character is too strong for your dislike of prison. Notice I do not say fear.

There is not much in this world that you are afraid of.'

Blimey mate, thought Callan. How wrong can you get?

'In that respect at least you are like Lonely. Not the fear, of course. I mean that you would sooner do another job and take your chance than continue as a petty clerk.'

Amateur psychologist, thought Callan. Knows it all. Even knows how he's going to handle me. He isn't even afraid of the gun any more.

'Go on,' he said.

'Naturally I am interested in you,' said the Greek. 'From what I learned about you it seemed you had a great potential–'

'And you were going to take a commission?'

'I was.'

'How much? Half?'

'I had thought of thirty-three per cent as a reasonable figure.'

'And what would I get out of it?'

'The opportunity to make a living in the way you prefer. A little help, when it was needed. I had thought of protection, for example.'

'You still thinking of it?'

'No,' the Greek said. 'Or rather not in the

same way.'

'A bit dodgy for you now, isn't it?'

'Dodgy? I don't think so. Why should it be dodgy?'

'I might kill you,' said Callan.

'What possible good would that do?'

'You saw me commit a murder,' Callan said. 'You're a witness. The only witness.'

'I saw you fight in your own defence against a man much bigger than yourself. I thought it admirable.'

'Like that is it?'

'It could be. By the way, where did you learn your karate?'

'I went to evening classes,' said Callan. 'Belt up and let me think.'

'Before you do so, there is one more fact to consider. Arthur is dead.'

'Let me know where to send the wreath.'

'I concede that these black comedy re-marks are an emotional release to you, but they do waste time,' said the Greek. 'Arthur was very useful to me. I need a successor.'

'Arthur's dead, long live Arthur?'

'You could be the man I need,' the Greek said.

'Yeah,' said Callan. 'Till I put this down.'

He rested the magnum's barrel on the table. It pointed at the Greek's stomach.

'If you accepted the job, you wouldn't have to put it down,' said the Greek.

'I don't work people over.'

'We can always hire someone for the rough work. What I need is a bodyguard. I paid Arthur five thousand a year. One hundred pounds a week. Tax free of course. You have already shown that you're superior to Arthur, and I therefore offer you more. One-fifty a week to start with. After six months we could consider an increase. All expenses paid of course. And all entertainment – including women. And of course alcohol – in moderation, I'm afraid. Even the best bodyguard is useless if he's drunk.'

'All this just to keep me alive?' Callan said.

'Believe me,' the Greek said, 'you would earn it. Every penny. Would you like a little more whisky?'

'No,' said Callan.

'May I – while you consider my offer?'

His hand reached out before Callan could answer. He was that sure of himself.

Callan said at last, 'It isn't enough. I can make more on my own.'

'How much more?'

'Fifty thousand quid,' said Callan. 'One night's work. Not much risk, either.'

'And yet you have a gun.'

'I like guns,' said Callan. 'They help me not to be embarrassed when I talk to people like you.'

'Suppose I let you do the job and keep the money – and cut you in on other jobs later?'

'Suppose I kill you?'

'You will then have two bodies to dispose of. If you leave me here, the police will find a magnum bullet in me – and they'll trace it eventually.'

Callan said nothing, only looked at his left hand, the fingers in position for a spear-strike.

'I've studied karate too,' said the Greek. 'I don't say I would beat you, but it would be very dangerous for you to find out.'

Callan said, 'Get me a glass of water.'

'If you are going to work with me I should prefer you to say please.'

'Get me a glass of water.'

The Greek shrugged, went to the sink and ran the water until it was cold.

Callan made his voice pleading. 'I don't say I won't come in, but it's a big decision,' he said.

That was better. When the Greek brought the water he was smiling. He offered the glass to Callan, bending forward from the hips, and Callan realized that at one time in his career the Greek had been a waiter.

Callan took the glass left-handed, and as he did so brought up the Noguchi, laid it alongside the Greek's jaw, the muzzle clipping neatly into the nerve-end. Arthur didn't have a monopoly on it after all. Not any more. He watched, the magnum in one hand, water-glass in the other, as the Greek pitched sideways to the floor, then sipped the water, and searched, first the Greek, then Arthur. The Greek was unarmed, which surprised Callan. Arthur carried a cosh of plaited leather and a Webley 380 Mark II revolver – Second World War vintage. That didn't surprise Callan at all. He opened the Webley, took the shells out of it and wondered what to do next. There was always the Greek's offer. Very tempting that. Good steady work, and a hundred and fifty quid every Friday. The only trouble was he couldn't do it. And now wasn't the time to start wondering why... He knew what dear old Toby would have done. Killed the Greek. Here and now. Just like that. But he couldn't do that either. Not after Arthur, not twice in one night, and the second one unconscious. Anyway the Greek might have left evidence about somewhere – he wasn't the kind to spend all his life in a garage – and if he had, the evidence had to be found, and you don't get inform-ation out of a dead man. Not that that was a reason: just an excuse.

There was a telephone on the sideboard, an extension to the one in the garage. Callan picked it up and dialled the number he could never forget.

'Hullo?' she said. Her voice was cool and yet enticing, like an ad for a refined sort of toilet soap.

'You're working late,' said Callan.

'Who is speaking, please?' The enticement had gone this time, but the coolness had intensified.

'All right,' said Callan, and recited the for-mula. 'This is Callan. Let me speak to Charlie please.'

'Charlie's asleep.'

'Don't be daft,' said Callan. 'Charlie's a robot. Plug him in love. This is urgent.'

Charlie was very very displeased when they woke him, and inclined at first to write off the whole deal. But Schneider's case was urgent, and the fact that Callan could be roaming around loose with a magnum revolver was not one to ignore. He promised to send a collecting van, and told Callan to come in with it, Callan yawned and stret-ched, then stowed the Webley and its shells in his attaché case. The Webley was far from his favourite gun, but it was better than no gun at all. When he'd finished he locked the case again, then suddenly it hit him. There was an icy sweat on his forehead, his knees shook, and he just got to the sink in time. He clung to its edge, retching, then vomited until his stomach was empty, until all that came up was bile. There was one more paroxysm, and he knew it was the last. When it was over, he turned and looked at the Greek. Still out. Callan knew he was lucky. If the Greek had come to while he was being sick, he, Callan, would have had no chance at all. He cleaned up the sink (it wouldn't do to let any contact of Hunter's know he had a nervous stomach) then took off the Greek's tie, and Arthur's, and used them to tie the Greek's hands and feet. After that he drank a little water, and kept it down. He longed for whisky, but that would only make him sick again, and anyway he daren't risk any more whisky.

It would be quite a wait, he knew. First they'd have to find out the address of this place from the telephone number he'd given them, then drive all the way across London. He looked at his watch. Jesus. Almost midnight already. Before a job he always liked an early night. He couldn't sleep much, but if you did the relaxing exercises you'd been taught, you were ready to cope next day. He rubbed his belly; it was aching again, but this time it wasn't sickness, just the thumping Arthur had given him. He sat down and made his muscles go loose, easy, following the relaxation drill. As it became automatic, he allowed his mind to move to the subject of Schneider, and how he would kill him.

At twelve-twenty a horn hooted outside his door three times. Callan looked at the second hand on his watch, and after twenty seconds the horn hooted again: two short, two long. Callan took out the magnum and went into the garage, put on the lights, then pressed the button for the door and took cover by the side of one of the trucks. As the door swung open, Toby Meres stood framed in the rectangle of light. He was dressed as an ambulance driver, and behind him stood a couple of ambulance attendants, with stretchers. Callan stepped into the light and put away the Noguchi.

'How very sweet of you,' said Meres. 'You remembered how much I like to be wakened up as soon as I've gone to sleep.' Callan led the way into the room behind the garage. The Greek had started to come round, and was trying to sit up. Meres hit him casually, his mind on other things, and he collapsed once more. Callan felt sick again.

The two ambulance attendants loaded the Greek on to a stretcher and took him out. Meres walked over to Arthur, and whistled softly.

'This must be your biggest yet,' he said. 'He'll weigh two hundred and fifty pounds at least. I should have him stuffed if I were you.'

'Belt up,' said Callan. His whole body wanted to shiver, and it took all his concentration of mind to prevent it.

'What blows did you use?' Meres asked.

'Three finger strike to the gut, chop to the jaw, then a throat punch.'

'Which one killed him?'

'They all did,' Callan said wearily. 'That's why we learned to use them.'

'I did it once,' said Meres. 'I used a spear strike. Didn't quite time it right. The bloke died in hospital.'

The stretcher bearers came in again, and picked up Arthur. He was almost too much for them, and they complained about it. On the way to headquarters, Callan, as friend of the bereaved, rode inside with the stretcher bearers. They didn't talk much, and spent a lot of time looking at Callan's hands. Meres used the two-note siren more than was necessary. He found the noise of it pleasing.

CHAPTER TEN

'It's a very awkward situation,' said Hunter.

He looked fit and relaxed, as if he'd slept deeply for eight hours. It was one-thirty a.m.

'Not my fault,' said Callan. 'You told me to get a gun.'

'I didn't tell you to start a massacre.'

Callan rubbed his stomach again. The doctor on duty had told him it was O.K., but his stomach didn't believe it.

'It was either start one or be one,' said Callan.

'And you're traced. Your address is known,' Hunter said. 'You could be blown at any time.'

'Only the Greek's people know where I am,' said Callan. 'Maybe only one of them. And anyway – I'll move after the job.'

'It's untidy,' Hunter said. 'It leaves loose ends – and you know how much I dislike that. Dear boy, I think we may have to postpone the job for a little while.'

'You're taking me off it?'

'Indeed no. You're going to do it – after I've done something about the Greek... A pity you didn't kill him too.'

'I thought about it,' said Callan. 'Then I remembered how much you hate loose ends.'

'On balance I think you were right,' said Hunter. 'Of course he may still have to die eventually. We'll see. But that can wait till Garstang's seen him.'

'Garstang?'

'He's new,' Hunter said. 'A psychologist. Interrogation specialist. Rather good, in an off-beat way. I think you'd better go home now. Unless you'd like some bacon and eggs. I daresay someone could – "rustle them up". Isn't that the expression?'

'Thanks,' said Callan. 'I'm not hungry.'

'Somehow I didn't think you would be,' said Hunter.

He was dog-tired when he got home, but the sleep he needed didn't come easily. Of course there were ways: a brew of tea, whisky, the supply of pills he'd hoarded against the emergency that so far hadn't come. But the whisky or the pills were an admission of defeat, and to get up and brew tea demanded strength of will he didn't have any more, not after what he'd done to Arthur. It was better – it was *essential* – to lie in bed, lie very still in the dark with the blankets pulled up to his neck: lie there and play out a battle in his mind. This time he chose Fuentes d'Onoro, seeing the struggle between Wellington and Masséna as an enormous game of chess, and when the casualties came – French chasseurs, British infantry who had failed to form square in time – they were only model soldiers after all: beautifully and exactly made, perfectly to scale, but lifeless. That was the important thing. They had never lived, so how could they possibly die?

When he did fall asleep, he dreamed at once of Donner. It was a nightmare he knew, and dreaded, with the last remnant of his conscious mind. But always the nightmare was too strong for him. He'd never wakened from it: he doubted that he ever would. It began with the fact that Donner had been a good man. The definition of that word 'good' had never even occurred to Callan until he met Donner and afterwards it became unnecessary. A good person was one who resembled Donner; there was no need to pursue the definition more closely. Besides being good, Donner had also been likeable, and this had made him unique in

Callan's experience. Before Donner, the good people in his life had been prison chaplains, prison visitors, an immense and totally unlovable great-aunt who had played the trumpet in a Salvation Army band. Donner was like none of these.

He was an American; a cheerful and successful newspaper columnist who wrote a political column valued for its wit, its accuracy and its firm commitment to moral standards, even in contemporary politics. The column had never been an overwhelming success, but it had done well enough for Donner to meet and talk freely with secretaries of state, admirals, generals and ambassadors, And Donner travelled a lot. His readers liked it when they picked up their newspapers in Des Moines, Jersey City, Oswego, and read that Donner was still at it, hammering away at the same moral issues in Tokyo, or Buenos Aires, or West Berlin. Maybe it was the fact that there were moral issues to be hammered at in places so far away from Washington that gave their readers comfort. And wherever his date-line was, Donner continued to meet presidents, ministers, admirals, generals, ambassadors. He attended the dinners and the cocktail-parties, drank and made jokes and listened to the gripes of the great, and never once printed anything that he'd been told off the record. Then he came to London, and the situation was as it had always been.

Callan never knew how Hunter had got on to him. Donner had stayed at the Hilton, and of course Hunter had the place bugged once there'd been a suspicion, but the bugging told very little Hunter didn't know already. Donner had been spying for Russia for seven years. As a spy he was immensely valuable to the KGB. He never got them much technical stuff, but that wasn't his function. Dormer's areas of specialization was the stresses and strains of the great: who drank, who took pills, who looked for oblivion in gambling, or women, or men. All the little weaknesses that were revealed at the dinners and cocktail parties, the things that Donner had promised never, never to use, and never did use: merely passed on to his controller. It had been his goodness that got him in to it. They'd set him up very nicely when Donner had been a foreign correspondent in West Berlin; an investment that paid off splendidly when he'd been given a column of his own. He'd told Callan all about it on the night Callan killed him: gabbling it all out as if he believed that Callan couldn't possibly shoot so long as

Donner went on talking.

They used a girl, and she must have been good, but then their women usually were good, particularly the ones who'd been trained at their star college in Bykovo, forty miles outside Moscow. They'd met at a party, in the days before the Berlin Wall, and she'd become his mistress. Later she'd told him that her family were still in East Berlin, and her father was an officer in the Volkspolizei, the Vopos, perhaps the most detested police in Europe. She'd fed him some information, small stuff, but useful, the kind that did him a lot of good with his editor. He told her about his plans to be a columnist, and asked her to marry him. She had wept and said how much she loved him, but marriage was impossible. She already had a husband, a Catholic, in East Berlin, and he'd never agree to divorce. Then she became pregnant, and went back to East Berlin to beg her husband to release her. She'd been back across the border for three hours when the Vopos got her. The next day they sent for Donner.

After that it was all so routine they could have sung it in four part harmony; but Donner didn't know that. To Donner it was all horrifyingly new. Frau Schacht had been interrogated. So far she had refused to incriminate Donner, but there was none the less evidence to show that she had participated in acts hostile to the German Democratic Republic, including the purveying of tendentious material to Donner. Then they had let him see her, and she hadn't looked too bad, but he'd got the feeling they'd hurt her, though she hadn't said so. She was a damned brave kid. Or so he thought. He'd asked what would happen to her, and they'd told him, matter of factly, that she would be shot. He'd begged and pleaded, and they'd watched him like Pavlovian doctors, observing an animal doing the things it had been conditioned to do. There had been no hint of a deal. There was no mention of a deal for five more days, and when it came, Donner believed till the moment that Callan shot him, that he had suggested it.

In the end they said they would let her live, in exchange for the information that Donner gave them. He was told that she was in prison, but mildly treated, and when the time came, that her child was born, and Donner believed he had a son. Three times he was shown photographs of her and the child, but not allowed to keep them: four times messages from her were played to him on a tape-recorder and he was allowed to record a reply. It never occurred to Donner that the pictures and tapes invariably occurred at the time of his unconscious questioning of her situation, or his unwillingness to go on. Always the knowledge of her existence, the fear of her future, and his son's, was enough. Donner obeyed his masters for nine years – but at the end of it Hunter got the last, faint trace of a scent, and being Hunter, that was enough.

Frau Schacht had never been to prison, nor was she pregnant. Instead, she'd gone to North Africa, where she had done some excellent work as a K.G.B. operator for a time. But in Tangier she'd acquired a taste for kif, and kif made her talkative. Her supplier was a Greek who freelanced for M.I.6, and once she mentioned Donner's name. The information, in due course, reached Hunter. He'd had Donner in a yellow file at once, and got on to the C.I.A. The C.I.A. was negative, all the way through, but Hunter had persisted, and turned up a British military attaché at Bonn who'd shot himself three weeks after he'd been to a very drunken party. He left card debts of fifteen thousand pounds. Donner had also been to the party...

In London it was Donner's business to find out about Charlock. Charlock was a banker of genius, seconded to the Treasury, who had twice pulled back Great Britain from the very brink of devaluation. His one relaxation was going to bed simultaneously with a boy and a girl, and Charlock liked them young. Hunter made no moral judgments about it: Charlock's hobby was a fact of insignificant size when set against the enormous fact of his ability to shore up his country's economy. Hunter spotted the target, and put Callan on to it. Callan followed Donner to the flat of a girl whose passport said she was an actress. There was no record of her having appeared on any stage or screen. After they had made love, the actress told Donner about Charlock, and she was in a position to know. She had once made up a third of the undertaking. Callan had picked him up outside the flat, and taken him to a tenement in Bayswater, a known haunt of prostitutes and there Donner had gabbled away as if his voice alone could keep him alive, and in the end had broken down and wept, then made a break for it, and Callan had shot him dead, one bullet through the heart, fired from a Smith and Wesson 38 Combat Masterpiece revolver with a four-inch barrel. Afterwards, Callan had removed from the corpse Donner's wallet, travellers' cheques, gold Dunhill lighter and Piaget wristwatch. The corpse had remained undiscovered for almost a day, and afterwards the police had interviewed hundreds of prostitutes and scores of pimps, but none had owned, or even borrowed a Smith and Wesson 38 Combat Masterpiece revolver. Donner's epitaphs were guardedly salacious leaders in cheap newspapers, but Hunter did not consider that germane to the issue. Besides, the C.I.A., when the thing was explained to them, were extremely grateful...

The nightmare always began at the tenement in Bayswater. By then he'd picked up Donner in a car, and he and the driver had got him inside. At first he'd thought it was a gag – a publicity stunt, or some new real life situation show for TV – then he'd thought of robbery, then kidnapping. It was only when the driver had left that he'd been really afraid: only then that the idea of Frau Helga Schacht first occurred to him, and then he'd begun to talk. In the nightmare all this was speeded up, but it slowed down as he began to cry, and still crying, ran to the door. Then Callan fired, and the bullet hit where it was supposed to, and Donner fell to the floor and went on crying, and Callan fired again and again, until all six cylinders were empty. And each time, before he fired, Donner called out

'Please', and it was the same each time Callan reloaded, and fired another six rounds. And another six. And another. And another. Please. Please. Please. Please. Please. Please.

Jenny said, 'Wake up.'

She had been saying it for some time, and Schneider found that she was clinging to him, her arms round his shoulders as she shook him. There was, as always, the hideous split second when he didn't know who he was, or she was, or even what country he was in, and then the familiar contact of her body told him: 'You are Schneider. I am Jenny. We are in bed together in a house in Hampstead, a house I nag you about because I think you paid too much money for it.'

'You're insatiable,' said Schneider.

'You only say that because I don't know what it means.'

'It means that you want me to make love to you, even though I'm a middle-aged man who should be sleeping.'

'Sleep then,' said Jenny, 'but don't make such a fuss about it.'

'I never fuss,' said Schneider.

'You were fussing then. You were having a nightmare.'

'I only have nightmares when I'm awake,'

Schneider said.

'It was all in German,' said Jenny. 'You were shouting like a soldier. An officer. At first you were very brave and nasty' – Schneider winced – 'but afterwards you were afraid and I loved you.'

'You don't speak German. How do you know I was afraid? Or nasty?'

'I know everything about you,' said Jenny. He put his arms about her.

It must have been the Caucasus, Schneider thought. That time in 'forty-two, in the first snows, when that tank appeared and wiped out my whole company, and those Uzbeks came up behind the tank and killed the survivors. Maybe their ammunition had been low, or maybe they just enjoyed their work; whatever the reason they'd used rifle butts and bayonets, not bullets.

'What do you mean you have nightmares when you're awake?' Jenny said.

The clatter of the tank, the sounds of killing receded.

'Are you worried about Noguchi?' Jenny asked.

'I am worried about nothing,' said Schneider. 'Why should I worry about twenty thousand pounds?'

'I don't know,' said Jenny. 'But you do

worry about it.'

'Our last deal,' said Schneider. 'When it is over I will have two hundred thousand sterling. Once my target was a quarter of a million, but that is too much. Two hundred thousand is quite enough for us to enjoy ourselves, and to take care of you when I'm gone.'

'I don't like you to talk like that,' she said.

'But it's necessary to talk like that.'

'No!'

She tried to sit up, to face him, but he held her down, his hands intuitively gentle.

'It is very necessary,' he said. 'I love you. It is my duty to take care of you.'

She lay still then, and her very stillness drew him to her, her body unfurled to him. When they had done, she said, 'I think you should play soldiers again.'

'Why should I do that?'

'Your mind is too full of real wars,' said Jenny, and her fingers rubbed the back of his neck, easing him, relaxing him, until he fell asleep, though she did not.

CHAPTER ELEVEN

Going to work was another nightmare. He was exhausted, his stomach was still sore, the underground was packed with people like himself, crammed into mobile metal containers that would hurtle them towards eight hours of misery and insult so that they could sleep late on Sundays. And at the end of it there was Waterman: greedy and suspicious as ever, and already regretting his pay rise, which Callan was obviously squandering on booze and women – or why would he come to work exhausted? Doggedly Callan attacked ledgers, invoices, pay-in slips, but that day the balance, that usually came to him so easily, was as unwilling as a virgin. It had to be sought, longed for, pursued; and so Callan wooed it, grateful, despite his weariness of mind. It stopped him thinking of Donner.

At twelve thirty, Waterman left, eager for gin, and at twelve thirty-five the phone rang. Callan scooped it up.

'Waterman's Ltd.'

'Charlie wants to speak to you,' she said, in

a voice so beautiful that only money could excite it. 'Is it convenient?'

'You know it is, love,' said Callan. 'Put him on.'

A pause, then Hunter said, 'You remember my instructions, Callan?'

'Yes,' Callan said. 'Not today.'

'Precisely,' said Hunter. 'Those instructions stand. But I think you ought to see your odoriferous little friend. Rebuke him a little. He did rather let you down. Unless you'd sooner Toby did it?'

'No, I'll handle it,' Callan said.

'As soon as it's convenient, I do hope?'

'When I finish tonight?'

'That will do admirably. Then come in and see me. I've something to show you. We might have a bit of dinner together.'

Then he hung up, and Callan went on with his pursuit of the balance, working through his lunch hour, dogged, obstinate, unwearying, the most inflexible of wooers, the kind who always wins in the end because the adored object is touched by such constancy, or flattered by it, or simply too tired to struggle any more.

The balance yielded at five-fifteen, half an hour after Waterman had left, and Callan put his head down on his desk and slept for forty minutes without a dream. When he woke he put away his books, tidied the office so that Waterman could wreck it next morning, then locked up. As he turned to leave, he saw Schneider watching him from his doorway. Schneider was smiling.

'Good evening, Mr. Schneider,' Callan said, and Schneider replied at once like an echo.

'Good evening, Mr. Callan.' The smile broadened, and he said, 'You remind me of a piece in the Bible.'

'Really?'

Callan knew he sounded bewildered. He felt he had every right to do so.

'Well done thou good and faithful servant. Have you a moment?'

'I should think so,' said Callan, and as he spoke Schneider stood away from the door, invited him in with a beckoning gesture. Like so many of his movements it was overdone, almost a send-up, but there was no mockery in it. Everything about Schneider, his speech, his movements, even in so trivial a matter as inviting Callan into his office, was designed to portray his enormous zest for life, and the happiness he got from it. For the first time, Callan realized how much he envied Schneider.

He went ahead of him, into the office, and moved at once to the table in the corner. The Talavera set-piece was still there. 'May I offer you some whisky?' Schneider asked.

'Just a small one,' said Callan.

'A small one,' said Schneider, as if he doubted his ability to pour such a measure.

The decanter he used was of crystal, and the whisky he poured into crystal tumblers was a pale colour, like straw. Callan took the glass he offered, and sniffed. It was a straight malt – Glen Grant maybe, or Glenfiddich. Three quid a bottle at least.

'Would you like some water?' Schneider asked.

'No thank you,' said Callan. 'This is fine as it is.'

'I think so too,' said Schneider, and raised his glass. 'Your health, Mr. Callan.'

'Yours,' said Callan, and both men sipped. From down the corridor Callan heard the sound of a door slammed, the rattle of keys.

That'll be Chalmers, he thought. F. R. Chalmers – Philatelist. Rare Stamps Bought and Sold. He's always the last one to leave the building. Schneider old love, there's only the two of us now. If Hunter hadn't changed his mind you could be dead in five minutes.

'As you see,' said Schneider, 'it is still Talavera. I have been too busy to set up a new battle. Besides, a man should not allow his hobby to intrude into his business. This' – he gestured at the table – 'is for relaxation only.'

'Relaxation?'

'It was in no sense a satisfactory battle,' said Schneider. 'The French were in a muddle from beginning to end. Marshal Jourdan quarrelled with King Joseph and each blamed the other when he lost. Nor was Wellington – Sir Arthur Wellesley as he then was – precisely at his best.'

'He had his Spanish allies to contend with,' said Callan. 'They were as big a menace as the French. And he made the French retreat – and they outnumbered him two to one.'

'Oh, he *won*,' said Schneider. 'He won handsomely. With Wellington, it was a habit. But it wasn't a pretty battle. Aesthetically it was not pleasing. The glorious march of the Light Brigade and the Horse Artillery, for example. They arrived too late. In a movie they would have got there just in time to save the day. Like this.'

He went to the table, and began to demonstrate. Callan found his ideas spectacular, even brilliant, but vulnerable to the cautious logicality of his own approach to war. At the end of an hour they were still arguing, still manoeuvring horse, foot and artillery. Callan could not remember when he had last enjoyed himself so much. At last Schneider said, 'I am afraid I must go now.'

Callan thought of Lonely. It was time that he left too.

'I've enjoyed this very much,' he said.

'I also. I should very much like to do it again, when we have more leisure. Sunday perhaps? At my house? We dine at eight, then we will have the night before us.'

'Thanks very much,' said Callan.

'You will not mind if my – wife leaves us after dinner? She has no taste for war.'

'Of course not,' said Callan.

'Good,' said Schneider. 'Till Sunday then.'

'Good night, Mr. Schneider.'

Callan had reached the door when he heard Schneider chuckle. He turned.

'Mr. Callan, you have forgotten something,' said Schneider.

'Have I?'

'Indeed you have. You should say to me, "Excuse me, Mr. Schneider, but I do not know your address."'

Callan said, 'Excuse me, Mr. Schneider, but I do not know your address.'

Schneider chuckled again. 'I think you

have just made a very English joke,' he said.

'I think so too,' said Callan.

'Eden House, Paradise Road, Hampstead,' Schneider said. 'That is an English joke also. Which battles shall we fight?'

'I leave it to you,' said Callan.

'I suggest we have two,' said Schneider. 'You will choose one and I will choose one, but neither of us tells the other till Sunday. O.K.?'

Callan said, 'I'll look forward to it.'

'I really believe you will,' said Schneider.

After that, it was time to call on Lonely. He wished it could have been the other way about. Matching his wits against Schneider was something he would have looked forward to, particularly when he thought of what he had to do. Rebuke him a little, Hunter had said. Usually when Hunter wanted someone rebuked you did it with a rubber hose – but Lonely had been kind to him, he'd even offered to refuse his commission. On the other hand he had been careless. Some kind of rebuke was merited. Callan set off to Lonely's Aunty Mildred's.

She had the first floor of a house near the King's Road, a neat piece of English domestic architecture in the style of Adam, *circa*

1780. The first floor alone must have cost ten thousand quid, Callan thought. What was it they said about brasses? Sitting on a fortune? Aunty Mildred must have sat to some purpose. He walked slowly past the house, and from an open window he could hear a voice raised in rebuke. The voice was female, its vocabulary basic but devastating, its theme that lazy nephews should bestir themselves and contribute to the expenses of aunts who found rates and taxes an appalling burden. A male voice, Lonely's, tried to intervene, but the aunt was off again, this time on the sexual habits of her income tax collector. Callan found them bizarre. He crossed the road and stood at a bus stop by a pub. It was as good a place as any for watching the house.

After ten minutes Aunty Mildred appeared. She looked like the kind of English gentlewoman who comes up from the country to shop twice a year at Harrods: all cashmere and tweeds and low-heeled, hand-lasted shoes. Only the cigarette in her mouth spoiled the effect. She swept past Callan and into the pub, where Callan heard her greeted with respect, even deference. He crossed the road then, and waited in the area below the stairs that led into the house. Within minutes

Lonely came down the stairs, and gave the road that careful scanning that petty crooks always use, and like all the other petty crooks, he forgot to look in the area. He was almost past it when Callan spoke.

'I want you,' he said.

Lonely shot up into his raincoat like squeezed toothpaste in a tube, then he turned, warily, as Callan walked up the area steps.

'Mr. Callan,' he said. 'You did give me a turn.'

'I want a word with you,' said Callan.

'I can't, Mr. Callan,' said Lonely. 'Not now. I got a job to do. Me Aunty Mildred–'

'She's in the boozer,' said Callan. 'I saw her go in. That's a very classy lady.'

'Bossy,' said Lonely. 'Brasses is always bossy – even when they've retired. That's why I can't stop and talk, Mr. Callan. She says it's time I did a job.'

Callan said, 'It's urgent, Lonely. Let's go inside.'

'What, in her place?' Lonely was appalled. 'She won't let none of my friends in her place.'

'Then we won't tell her,' said Callan. 'Get a move on, son. I haven't got all night.'

Lonely was still reluctant, but the threat in

Callan's voice was too much for him. He went back upstairs and unlocked the door, and Callan followed him in, up a superb staircase carpeted in blue, then waited while Lonely unlocked a handsome and authentic mahogany door.

'A Judd lock,' said Callan. 'Aunty doesn't believe in encouraging burglars, does she?'

Lonely led the way inside, into a sitting-room furnished with eighteenth-century and early Victorian pieces. The carpet was Aubusson, the one oil-painting a Stubbs, but there were besides miniatures and pieces of pottery, elegant trifles in silver and a superb horse carved in jade. Callan picked it up and looked at it.

'Knows her stuff does Aunty,' he said.

'Mr. Callan.' Callan put the horse down and looked at Lonely. The little man's face was red, his voice was hoarse with embarrassment.

'You won't nick anything, will you?' he said at last.

'See this wet, see this dry, cross my heart and hope to die,' said Callan, and performed the ritual. Lonely at once looked relieved.

'You don't know what a strain it is keeping my hands off this stuff. I could get an even thousand just for the silver.'

'Why don't you?' Callan asked.

'My Aunty would kill me.' Lonely said simply. 'Sit down, Mr. Callan. Make yourself at home. I'd offer you a drink, only–'

'Only what?'

'The old bag won't allow me to touch it. She knows how much is in every bottle she's got.' He hesitated a moment, then said, 'What's the trouble, Mr. Callan?'

Callan said, 'How did you know it was trouble, Lonely?'

At once there came the smell.

'You went to the Greek, didn't you?' said Callan. Lonely looked astonished.

'How did you know that?' he asked.

'You were followed,' Callan said. 'You led him to me.'

'But that's impossible,' said Lonely. 'You know how careful I am, Mr. Callan.'

'I know how careful you should be. Only you weren't. You got the gun from a geezer called Arthur, didn't you?– And Arthur put a scare into you. Right?'

Lonely didn't answer, didn't even look, he was so frightened, and Callan's arm reached out, the hand under Lonely's chin, not hurting him, but making him look into Callan's eyes.

'I asked a question, Lonely,' Callan said.

'And I want an answer.'

Lonely looked, and shuddered at what he saw. Usually those pale eyes told you nothing – you had to watch the mouth to see what kind of mood Mr. Callan was in – but this time they were burning with a rage that was close to madness. The last time he'd seen those eyes like that was when there'd been the barny with the snout barons, back in the Scrubs.

'Yes, Mr. Callan,' Lonely said. 'Arthur scared me. But–'

'But nothing,' said Callan. 'Arthur was supposed to scare you. That's how the Greek had you followed back to my place.' His hand dropped. 'You got careless, old son.'

Lonely struggled to find the words that would explain how difficult it was for the little man to survive in a big man's world.

'That Arthur would scare anybody,' he said at last.

'Not any more,' said Callan.

Carefully, dreading the answer, Lonely asked 'Has something happened to him then?'

'Yeah,' said Callan. 'Something's happened to him.'

'Did you shoot him, Mr. Callan?'

'No,' said Callan. 'I hit him.'

'You?' said Lonely. 'You hit Arthur?'

The incredulity in his voice was obvious.

'Yes, me,' Callan said. 'I hit Arthur. And what's more he died of it.'

'You're kidding,' Lonely said.

'No.'

And that one word was enough. Suddenly Lonely realized that what Callan said was true. Arthur was an ex-wrestler, ex-boxer: he'd once sparred five rounds with a world heavy-weight champion. He was the biggest, strongest man Lonely had ever seen, and Callan had hit him and he'd died.

'Gawd,' said Lonely, then added, 'what about the Greek, Mr. Callan?'

'He's with some friends of mine,' Callan said. 'By now he's probably envying Arthur.'

Lonely longed to look away from those burning eyes, but dared not do so.

'Which brings me to our problem,' Callan said. 'Yours and mine.'

'What problem's that, Mr. Callan?'

'You,' said Callan.

'I ain't done nothing,' Lonely said. It was a sentence he had used since he was seven years old, and as always, when he said it, his voice was a whine. As always, too, when he said it he smelled, because he knew he lied.

'You were careless,' said Callan. 'You fingered me. My friends don't like it. They've got a job lined up, and it's big – my God it's big.'

'I thought you was a loner,' Lonely said.

'I am mate. When I get the chance,' said Callan. 'These friends of mine are too rough for me. You know what, Lonely? I'm scared of them. That's why I do what they tell me. You think I wasn't scared of Arthur? Of course I was. But I croaked him because my friends told me to. He was trying to stick his nose in.'

'I wouldn't do that, Mr. Callan,' said Lonely.

'Or you take the Greek,' said Callan unheeding. 'He's bent, but he's big time, isn't he? Got a Savile Row suit and a Merc 600 and Arthur for a bodyguard. Big stuff. He eats little fellers like you for breakfast. Right? And now my friends have got him – and you wouldn't believe what my friends are doing to him.'

'What, Mr. Callan?' No horror, no matter how terrible, was better than Lonely's own imagination.

'It's chemicals,' said Callan. 'Injections. Things that–' He broke off, as if unable to continue. 'I'd sooner be flogged, old son. Straight I would.'

'It hurts that much?'

'It's agony, mate,' said Callan, and Lonely shuddered. 'It's what they want to do to *you*.'

Lonely let out a wail of terrified frustration.

'But Mr. Callan,' he said. 'I don't know what you're doing. I don't even want to know.'

'You put the Greek on to us. You know we've got him. You know I croaked Arthur.'

'But I won't tell. You know I won't. I don't grass, Mr. Callan. I never go near the rozzers.'

'Maybe the Greek's got friends,' said Callan.

'He's only had Arthur, Mr. Callan,' Lonely said. 'Those other geezers – like those gits that followed me – he'd just hire them for one job. They won't know anything. Honest.'

Callan said, 'That's all right then. Because you wouldn't split on me – would you, son?'

'Course not,' said Lonely, and for the first time he smiled.

'All the same, these friends of mine want you to keep your mouth shut.'

'You can tell them they've got nothing to worry about,' said Lonely.

'I'll tell them all right. You got sense, son.'

Lonely smiled again, and suddenly Callan's

fingers moved in a scaled down version of the blow that had killed Arthur, the fingers stabbing at a spot just below the sternum, and Lonely fell to his knees, retching with an agony that was beyond bearing.

'I'm sorry,' Callan said. 'I really am sorry. But they said I had to, old son. Just so you wouldn't forget what happened to Arthur.'

He left then, and Lonely stayed on his knees, waiting for the pain to become bearable. When it did, he collapsed into a chair. Suddenly he realized that he had always hated Mr. Callan. But it made no difference. No difference at all. Mr. Callan was still the strong one.

CHAPTER TWELVE

'Nice of you to drop in,' said Hunter.

'I thought I was invited to dinner.'

'Of course you are,' Hunter said. 'How about a little dry sherry first?'

'How about a little Chivas Regal?'

Hunter sighed, unlocked a cupboard and came up with whisky and Amontillado. The glass he handed to Callan was generous enough.

'I've spoken to Lonely,' Callan said, then raised his glass. 'Cheers.' He sipped.

'Cheers,' said Hunter. 'I hope he listened.'

'He'll keep shtum all right.'

'Keep shtum? Please, Callan – no vernacular.'

'He'll remain silent,' Callan said.

'Because you told him to?'

'Because I hit him,' said Callan. 'Hit him once. In the belly. A three-finger strike. A sample of what he'll get if he takes to chatting.'

'I think that was wise,' said Hunter.

'Do you know, I hate myself?' Callan said.

208

'Do you find that odd at all?'

'Not in the least,' said Hunter. 'If any-thing, it's reassuring.'

'Is it really?'

'Of course. It shows me you haven't changed. You always hated yourself after you'd done something unpleasant. It's the way you're made, Callan.'

'I hurt him,' Callan said. 'I really hurt him.'

'Of course,' said Hunter. 'Otherwise what would be the point?'

Dinner was brought in then, served at Hunter's desk by a white-jacketed steward. Dinner was game soup, roast beef, goose-berry fool and a bottle of Chambolle Musigny. Callan accepted one glass and longed for whisky, and watched Hunter sail into his food with a kind of dainty greed. Not hungry, he forced himself to eat. Hunter missed nothing. Loss of appetite might be taken for squeamishness, and Hunter could get a lot of fun out of squeamishness.

'We've got rid of Arthur for you,' he said.

'Good,' said Callan. 'But you didn't really do it for me.'

'Of course we did,' said Hunter. 'You're no longer part of my section.'

'That's right,' Callan said. 'I'm a freelance. And you need me. That's why I belted

Lonely – and why you got rid of Arthur.'

Hunter smiled at a fragment of beef, under-done, succulent, the kind to give a Hindu nightmares.

'Have you any plans for Schneider's future?' he asked.

'Would Sunday be too early?'

'Sunday would be excellent. You can arrange it?'

'He's invited me to his place,' said Callan.

'I find that odd.'

'He likes playing soldiers. So do I.'

'You'll be alone?'

'He'll have the girl with him. And that chauffeur – George. Looks like a hard boy to me.'

'Oh, yes, George,' said Hunter. 'We've made a few inquiries about him. He's not exactly a novice to this business.'

'I want him taken care of.'

'Wouldn't it be simpler to kill Schneider in his office?'

'If he'd stay there till after six-thirty – yes. it would. But usually he doesn't.'

'Why six-thirty, Callan?'

'To give myself a chance to get away. Any-way, you wanted me to nick his life savings.'

'You could do it afterwards.'

'No,' Callan said. 'One job is enough. Sunday at his place – and you immobilize George.'

'You I take it will handle the girl?'

'She won't take much handling,' he said. 'She's in it.'

Callan thought of the neatness and order of Schneider's safe.

'You think so too?' said Hunter. 'But not too far in. This time the fright will be enough. Which reminds me – your friend Papadopoulos.'

Callan said, 'There's no point in my saying I don't fall in love with people who beat me up, is there?'

'None whatever,' Hunter said. 'Think about it some time. Anyway – your friend Papadopoulos has really been most co-operative. I told you I intended to let Garstang have him?' Callan nodded. 'It worked well. Really extremely well. I think we might trot along and take a peep – before our coffee and brandy.'

They walked along the institution corridors, past the music room and art room, to a door labelled 'Physics Lab'. Hunter spoke into a microphone above the door.

'Garstang, my dear fellow, is it convenient?'

The voice, precise and classless, replied at

once: 'Certainly.'

'I have the – er – other half of the problem with me,' said Hunter.

'Perfectly acceptable,' said the voice. 'Come in.'

Hunter opened the door and entered, and Callan followed him into a combination of fashionable surgery and casualty ward. Cardiograph machines, an encephelograph, a blood-pressure device, a Ferrograph tape-recorder, Rorschach apparatus, lined the room, neatly available. On a bed in one corner lay the Greek, flat on his back, breathing as if in sleep but with his eyes wide open. He made no move as Hunter and Callan entered. At a battered table in the centre of the room, a table that had once seen much of Newton's laws, and Boyle's, a man sat writing up notes, and continued to do so until Hunter and Callan stood in front of him. Garstang. A little over thirty, and already balding, running to fat, but not in the least worried about it: not worried about anything, because of his absolute faith in his own ability. He put down his pen at last, and looked at Callan, who put on his 'prisoner up in front of the governor face', the one that gave nothing away.

'You're Callan,' said Garstang.

'That's right.' said Callan. 'And you're Garstang.'

'I thought you'd have been bigger,' Garstang said.

'I never thought about your size at all,' said Callan.

Garstang ignored it as he ignored all irrelevance.

'The blows you struck that chap known as Arthur–' He broke off, and his eyes ran over Callan, appraising – 'It must be a very specialized technique.'

'Oh, it is,' said Callan. 'Would you care for a demonstration?'

'I'm sorry,' said Garstang. 'Am I being rude? It's not a thing I know a great deal about I'm afraid.' Hunter chuckled then: appreciative. 'We did an autopsy on Arthur, you know. Quite amazing what a man's hands can do.'

Callan looked over his shoulder at the Greek.

'Should he be in on this?' he asked.

'Papadopoulos? He's in a state of fugue – induced of course.' He noticed Callan's bewilderment. 'I've caused him to suffer loss of memory – in certain areas. Go on over to him.' Callan hesitated. 'Go on. He won't have the remotest idea who you are.'

Callan walked over to the bed and looked down at the Greek. The handsome, clever face had lost some of its cleverness.

'Hallo,' Callan said. 'You remember me?'

The Greek smiled. To Callan it seemed an innocent and touching smile.

'You and Arthur came for me. Remember?' said Callan.

The Greek said something in a language Callan did not understand. It was Callan's turn to smile: he did not think his smile was innocent. The Greek repeated his words, and Callan caught the anxiety in his voice. At once Garstang came to the bed and spoke more strange words, firmly, soothingly. The Greek laughed and at once resumed his slow and regular breathing. Garstang drew Callan away.

'At the moment he has forgotten how to speak English,' Garstang said.

'Lucky you speak Greek,' said Callan.

'I was stationed with the R.A.F. in Cyprus,' Garstang said. 'He finds my Cypriot accent amusing. That's why he laughed.'

'Are you going to keep him like this?' asked Callan.

'That depends on our chief here,' said Garstang, then added: 'He's perfectly happy you know. He thinks he's a waiter at the moment, in a hospital in Salonika.'

'What's he think is wrong with him?'

'What he calls a nervous stomach. A rather apt expression. He *is* nervous – and a dyspeptic. And he was once a waiter in Salonika.'

'What did you find out about him?' Callan asked.

Garstang looked at Hunter.

'Oh, you can talk in front of Callan,' Hunter said: 'He's in no position to reveal our secrets.'

'I rarely make moral judgments,' Garstang said, 'but Papadopoulos really is one of the most unpleasant people it's ever been my misfortune to meet.'

'In what way?' Callan asked.

'In every way. Morally, socially, sexually. Basically his driving force is greed: for sex, food, drink, money and above all power: power being a prerequisite of all the others. To achieve power he's willing to do anything. I mean that quite literally. Most of it's been the exploitation of other criminals – like yourself.'

Callan said to Hunter, 'You must really trust this one.' Garstang smiled.

'He's in a yellow file,' Hunter said. 'It doesn't seem to worry him unduly, does it, Garstang?'

'On the contrary,' said Garstang, 'I find it very useful – in terms of my field of study.'

Callan knew that Garstang meant it. The thought appalled him. 'Go on about Papadopoulos,' he said.

'He seems to have begun his career in Salonika as an agent-provocateur. He would join communist underground organizations, then betray them for money.'

'He had some nerve then,' Callan said. 'Most people who try that don't live long.'

'We all have nerve when we want something badly enough,' said Garstang. 'Besides, he's an exceptionally able man. When he'd accumulated some capital he moved to Athens, abandoned politics and turned to vice.' He looked at Hunter, who was laughing. 'Have I said something funny?' he asked.

'Yes,' Hunter said firmly. Garstang made a note.

'Vice paid better,' he continued. 'Prostitution provided a regular income, and homosexuality, and its contingent blackmail, produced irregular but satisfactory bonuses. Again after an accumulation of capital, he changed his base: this time to London. By then he had some contact with the British underworld, and he used it shrewdly. First he hired Arthur, then set up as a financier and supplier of petty criminals who wished to attempt tasks that were beyond their means. I had never realized until I talked to him that crime requires capital as much as any other business. Arthur's duty was to see that payment was made – occasionally over-payment.' He turned to Callan. 'Sometimes – as in your case – he would supply equipment then force the other party into sharing the enterprise with him. Did he hurt you?'

'Arthur did,' said Callan.

'Papadopoulos delights in hurting people,' said Garstang. 'Part of the garage you visited was equipped for that purpose. On balance I would say you were lucky.' He looked at his notes. 'I think that's all,' he said. 'Oh, yes. He estimates that he is worth half a million pounds. I suppose that's relevant?'

'Extremely,' said Hunter.

'Odd,' said Garstang. 'He lied about that right to the end – and when I got the truth out of him he wept. Do you have any questions?'

'Just one. How the hell did you get him to tell you all this?' Callan asked.

'No thumbscrews or anything of that kind,' said Garstang. 'It's essentially a sub-liminal technique – based largely on hallucinogen drugs and hypnosis.'

'Is it dangerous?'

'In what way?' Garstang asked.

Callan nodded at the smiling figure under observation in Salonika.

'To him.'

'Oh, extremely,' said Garstang. 'If we go on too long, that is. The drugs used are addictive, you see, and that means increasingly large doses. And *that* means his mind will be damaged irreparably – if we go on.'

'And will you go on?'

'That,' said Hunter, 'is my business. Good night, Garstang.'

'Good night to you,' said Garstang. By the time they reached the door he was back at his notes.

Hunter's coffee was excellent, and the brandy was something that Callan needed urgently. Sipping it, rolling it around in a rummer as custom prescribed, was almost as big an agony as not drinking at all. Garstang had terrified him even more than the Greek and Arthur had done. The Greek and Arthur were at least explicable, and given the opportunity could be dealt with by normal means: a fist, a bullet, a knife. But Garstang was something else again. That plump and sloppy pedant was doing things to the mind that

218

Callan dreaded, and the fact that the mind he was currently working on was evil had no significance. Garstang would just as cheerfully get inside a saint. Hunter was well aware of it.

'That chap's going to make your type redundant, Callan,' he said. 'If we ever devise a way of getting the subjects to him.'

'You could use robots for that,' said Callan.

'You speak of the ideal world,' said Hunter. 'Let's stick to the real.' Suddenly he began to laugh. 'When he had accumulated some capital he moved to Athens, abandoned politics and turned to vice,' he quoted. 'That's the sublime style, Callan. The simplicity of brilliance. It sounds like a sentence out of Caesar's Commentaries.'

'What are you going to do with him?' Callan asked.

'Garstang?'

'Papadopoulos.'

'Keep him, of course,' said Hunter. 'There's always a use for chaps like that.'

'He knows about me. He knows about the gun,' said Callan.

'That might be useful,' Hunter said. 'Wouldn't you say that might be useful?'

'You don't have to lean on me,' said Callan. 'I'm going to do this job. And another thing

– all that codology about hallucinogens and subliminal techniques to find out about the Greek – Lonely told me all I needed in three minutes.'

'May I ask why he told you?'

'Because he's scared of me,' said Callan. 'And I'm not proud of it.'

'He'd better go on being scared of you – for his own sake.'

'He will be,' Callan said. 'It's sort of natural with him – like breathing.'

'Let's talk about how you propose to kill Schneider,' said Hunter.

Callan began to talk, and Hunter leaned back in his chair, the tips of his fingers together, like a don at a tutorial: a don who knows that his pupil has an excellent chance of a first.

CHAPTER THIRTEEN

The problem was how to get hold of a tape-recorder. Hunter was having him watched round the clock, now that the job was so close. It was routine, and they both knew it. Moreover, all the advantage was with the watchers. It didn't matter whether Callan spotted them or not. Their business in life was simply to hang on and see what Callan was up to – and even if he did shake them, Hunter would call him in and find out what he'd been playing at, or send good old Toby and a few mates along to find out – and Callan didn't fancy that. But he'd got to get hold of a recorder, that was absolutely essential.

It was funny, he hadn't thought about it that way, not at first. When Hunter had first sent for him it had all been great. He'd never felt better, or easier in mind. It was a chance to get back, to do the job he could do better than anybody else – and let's face it, somebody had to do. It was a war, like Hunter said, and Callan knew enough about wars not to have any illusions about fair play, 'you fire first' and International Courts at the Hague. In wars you clobbered the other bloke and if he wasn't looking when you fired all it meant was your chances were that much better. So he'd wanted to get back in: he wanted to kill Schneider. Still did, if it came to that. Schneider was at war too. The only difference between them was that Schneider didn't know where the enemy was.

But going back to Hunter's section, that was different. He didn't fancy that now. Hunter had shown him too much. Not just Toby – all right. Toby liked killing people, but every regiment had a few of *them* – it was that bleeder Garstang and the things he got up to. Callan couldn't understand why, not really, but Garstang had revolted him, and Hunter must have known it, yet Hunter had let him see Garstang at work. The question was why? As a threat maybe? 'You see what I can do, Callan. You carry out orders or you'll get the same.' That was likely enough, knowing Hunter. Or maybe it was part of something else. Maybe Callan wasn't going back to Hunter's section: maybe Hunter had never intended he should, and Callan had been taken along to see Garstang so the psychiatrist could prepare the Greek for the evidence he would give at the trial. The trail was as wide as a motorway, after all. Ballistics expert to identify the gun, the Greek to say he'd supplied it to Lonely, and Lonely to tell the world he'd given it to Callan. Callan had no illusions about Lonely. He'd keep quiet only as long as Callan was loose. Once he was safe in the nick, Lonely would squeal his head off, particularly after Callan had belted him.

And it would be no good Callan telling the rozzers he'd killed Schneider because he was working for an executive section of M.I.6. Even if they believed him enough to go to the headquarters, all they'd find would be Vic and a bloody great pile of scrap-metal. No TV sets, no firing range, no Garstang and no Greek. And then there was Schneider's girl. They'd have her too, and the story of the money that Callan had nicked after he'd blasted her boyfriend. His Lordship the Judge would love that one. 'Mr. Cadwallader, is the prisoner attempting to persuade us that our country's secret service empowered him not only to murder but to steal on their behalf?'

'That is his submission, my lud.'

'Has your client been examined by a competent alienist, Mr. Cadwallader? I take it he *is* entering a plea of diminished responsibility?' Laughter in court. Oh yes, go down great, that would.

Callan knew that if he was nicked he hadn't a prayer. Of course in a way that had been true of every job he'd done. All that crap you read about. If you get caught you're on your own. Well it wasn't crap. It was true. The only thing was if you had the section behind you, you didn't get caught. They got you out. But this time he didn't know whether he had the section behind him or not. This time Hunter might be killing two birds with one stone – getting rid of Schneider, and Callan. Because a Callan roaming around loose was always a potential threat to Hunter, and a Callan doing bird for murder and robbery wasn't, not till he came out, and for murder and robbery he'd be lucky if he got twenty years.

So just in case, Callan decided he had to have a bargaining factor, and the best he could dream up was a tape-recorder. Not much, but better than writing it down. He'd never been any good at putting things on paper. His strength was in talking things out, telling it in his own words, mimicking the rhythms and cadences of other people's speech. And anyway it would take him weeks to write this lot down, the stuff he had to tell not just about Schneider, but Donner too, and Naismith and Bunin. All of them. All the jobs he'd done. Every bloody one. In detail. It wasn't much of a chance, but it was the best chance he had. Only first he had to get hold of the thing, and that meant asking Lonely. It was true that last time they had met he had struck Lonely below the sternum and caused him a great deal of pain, hardly the best way to inspire willingness, but on the other hand Lonely was terrified of him. That was all that was needed.

He didn't have a chance to call the little man until lunch time, and even then he daren't use the office phone. It might be bugged. He couldn't go outside either. The men watching him would see him make the call, and Hunter would want to know who it was to. Instead he went up one flight of stairs to 'Rossiter and Phee (Fruit and Vegetables) Ltd.' He'd once been sweet on their typist (clammy gropings in newsreel cinemas, widowed mum in Peterborough, a smelly old cat who slept on her bed). She married a rep for a chocolate firm, but Callan had collected her from her office often enough to know that the lock on Rossiter and Phee's door was the easiest in the building. He knew too that nobody stayed in the office at lunch time.

Even with gloves on, the lock took less than a minute. He sat on the receptionist's desk and dialled the number of Lonely's Aunty Mildred.

By the eleventh ring, Callan was sweating, but he let it go on. At the twenty-fifth the receiver was lifted, and Lonely's angry voice said 'Hallo.' But even his anger was weak.

Callan said, 'This is Callan.' He waited, but there was no sound from the other end. 'How you feeling, son?'

'Got a bruise,' said Lonely. 'It's all purple. Hurts me when I walk upstairs.'

'You'll live,' said Callan. 'Where's Aunty Mildred?'

'In the kip. She was boozed last night,' Lonely said. 'Blimey, she can shift it.'

'I've got another job for you,' said Callan.

'No!' Lonely yelled so hard that Callan pulled the receiver from his ear, but there were no more words.

Callan said, 'Lonely – ask yourself one question. Are you being wise? I mean have you really thought about what might happen if you turn down this perfectly simple request?'

'All right,' Lonely said wearily. 'All right, Mr. Callan. What do I have to do?'

Callan told him, and when he'd finished

Lonely showed no surprise. Nothing that happened ever surprised him, only sometimes it hurt.

After the phone call Callan locked up Rossiter and Phee and went down to his own floor. A man was trying the door of Waterman's Ltd. Callan moved softly into the adjacent lavatory, flushed the toilet, and walked out briskly. The man had gone, but he picked up Callan in the foyer of the building, and followed him to the pub where Callan ate a sandwich and drank half a pint of bitter. At six o'clock there were two of them waiting for him. They followed him all the way to the King's Road, then into the Admiral Collingwood, the pub Lonely's aunt had used the night before. They were a couple of good ones, unobtrusive, clerkly men so lacking in interest as to be almost invisible. In the Admiral Collingwood, packed out with models, painters, actors, P.R. men, shop assistants, guardsmen and employees of the North Thames Gas Board, they promptly disappeared. Callan saw Lonely at the bar and squeezed his way towards him. As he drew near, Lonely turned, nursing a pint of bitter, flowed round a chubby A and R man, and bumped into Callan, who felt a slight increase in weight in the left hand pocket of his raincoat.

'Lonely,' he said. 'How nice. You're just the bloke I want to see.'

He noticed with relief Lonely's look of distress. It was genuine.

'Wait here,' he said. 'I'll be with you in a moment.'

Then it was his turn to fight his way to the bar and clamour for whisky. When he'd got it, he went back to Lonely and drew him into an unoccupied corner, but stayed a good two feet away. His two tails weren't near enough to hear anything, but they were watching.

'I put it in your pocket, Mr. Callan,' Lonely said.

'I know,' said Callan. 'Did you get the money?'

'Yes, ta, Mr. Callan. Ten quid. Just right.'

Callan felt the fury that his fear created boiling up inside him.

'You dozy nit,' he said. 'Did you take it out and count it?'

Lonely for once in his life looked scornful.

'Do me a favour,' he said. 'I took it out of your pocket and put it in mine. That's where I counted it, Mr. Callan. In my pocket.'

'Don't get cheeky,' said Callan.

'I'm sorry, Mr Callan,' he said. 'It's me stomach. It hurts.'

Callan willed himself not to apologize. And yet the little man had helped him, and even tried not to make money out of him.

'Better me than those friends of mine,' he said. 'Go to a chemist's. Get some arnica. Rub it on. That'll take the sting out of it.' He finished his whisky, then tapped one forefinger against Lonely's lips.

'Keep it buttoned,' he said.

'You can trust me, Mr. Callan,' said Lonely.

'I can do better than that, son,' said Callan. 'I can kill you. And those friends of mine – they can make you wish I had.'

He pushed his way out of the pub and the clerkly men escorted him to his door. Not once on the journey did Callan put his hand in his raincoat pocket. Instead, he read a paper. The pound was in peril, a cricket match had sparked off a riot in the West Indies, there was foot and mouth disease in Montgomeryshire and racial discrimination in the Midlands. Callan reckoned that, on balance, Schneider was the sanest man he knew. When he got back to his flat he dug out the books he needed for Sunday's battle. Schneider, he thought, would fight one of Wellington's. Callan set aside Sir Charles Oman's *History of the Peninsular War*, Guedalla's *Life of Wellington* and Sir Edward

Creasy's *Fifteen Decisive Battles in World History*. That would take care of Waterloo. Callan had decided on an American Civil War battle, probably Gettysburg. For that he would use the modern historians like Catton and Hansen, but even they wouldn't be needed all that much. What Robert E. Lee and George G. Meade had done on 1st and 3rd July, 1863, was as familiar to Callan as if he had been present, or even more familiar than that. What men do in the heat of battle they never clearly remember, but Callan had fought over Gettysburg a hundred times, with the aid of eye-witnesses, sociologists, historians, generals. Whichever side Schneider chose, Callan was confident of Gettysburg.

He moved across the flat once more, letting the watchers see him, then settled down to read. Five minutes after the opening salvos of Vittoria were fired, Callan's telephone rang. Callan put down his book, and picked up the phone, and His Grace of Wellington's battle-plan faded.

'Callan.'

'Charlie wants to speak to you,' he said.

'Then how can I refuse?' said Callan.

Hunter came through at once.

'So you went visiting this evening?'

'Yeah,' said Callan. 'I got to thinking about Lonely.'

'I thought you took care of him yesterday?'

'I thought so too,' said Callan. 'But I wanted to see what Lonely thought.'

'And what does he think?'

'His lips are sealed.'

'Excellent,' said Hunter. 'I hardly think it's worth while to bother him again, do you?'

'No,' said Callan. 'He'll do.' He yawned. 'You can send your watchdogs home, Hunter. I'm not going out again tonight.'

'They're for your protection,' Hunter said. 'You know how nervous I get before an operation.'

'You've no idea how well I'll sleep tonight,' said Callan.

'Oh, dear. Were they that bad?'

'They were good,' Callan said, 'but Gawd help them if they ever meet an Arthur.'

He hung up and went on with his reading, waiting for the daylight to dim so that he could draw the curtains. There could be other watchers: for what he was about to do he could take no chances.

Hunter said, 'You got a full report from those men watching Callan?'

'Yes, sir,' said Meres.

'A *very* full report?'

'He spoke to only one person, sir. Lonely.'

'And how did Lonely look after Callan spoke to him? Frightened?'

'Terrified, sir.'

'Did Lonely have any idea that Callan had come to see him?'

'They think not, sir. It seems that Lonely bumped into him. Quite literally.'

'Hmm,' said Hunter.

Callan drew the curtains at last, and took the tape-recorder from his waistcoat pocket. Lonely had done him proud all right.

It was a little beauty. Another Jap job. Transistorized. Not much bigger than a cigarette packet. Strictly speaking not a tape-recorder at all. A wire-recorder. Thirty minutes on the spool, and two spare spools. He could natter away his whole life story in the time that gave him. Pretty juicy too, some of it. Sunday newspaper stuff. He looked at his telephone. The odds, the very long odds, were that it was bugged by now. And nowadays they had bugs that picked up noises in a room even when you weren't using the phone. He could look at the phone of course, and find the thing, take it out, but if he did he'd tip his hand to Hunter anyway.

Callan sighed. He would have to go into the kitchen; not the cosiest of places. Then suddenly he cheered up. While he was about it he would have a bath.

'Dear boy,' said Hunter, 'when did we bug Callan's flat?'

'Tuesday, sir,' said Meres. 'His second evening at target practice.'

'Difficult to get in?'

'I sent our lock man, sir. He was most impressed. He thought that if he did anything to the lock on the door, Callan would know. He thinks that Callan designed the lock himself, sir. In the end he got in by the window, and even that wasn't easy.'

'The bug *is* functioning?'

'Yes, sir. So far there's been nothing to report. Nothing relevant that is.'

'Would it be too much trouble to ask you to go and listen now?'

'We do have a man on it, sir.'

'I'd like you on it,' said Hunter. 'Just for a little while. Then you can come back and tell me all about it.'

Callan sat on the edge of the bath as it filled, and talked softly into the wire-recorder. No matter how good the bug in his phone was, it would pick up nothing but the sound of running water. He talked quickly, scarcely looking at the notes he had made, and what he had to say was addressed to Detective Inspector Pollard and Detective Sergeant Grace of New Scotland Yard. They would know enough about murder to appreciate the significance of the detail he was offering them. Naismith. Bunin. Orthez. Megali. Donner. Bunin had put a bullet in him, so maybe that one was self-defence. Orthez had tried to ambush him, so he could try self-defence for that one too. Megali had used a knife, and he'd been quick with it: bloody quick. But Naismith, his first job, had been murder, and nothing else but – and so had Donner, his last. And it was no good his telling himself that Naismith was a bastard who deserved to die. It was still murder, murder of an evil man, just as the Donner job had been murder of a good one. Callan told them all, then went on to outline the Schneider plan: the way Hunter had set it up, planted Callan on Waterman so that he could be near to Schneider: the business of getting the gun – no mention of Lonely, but details of the price paid, the encounter with Papadolpoulos and Arthur (would Arthur's death too be counted as murder?):

the plan of attack, road drills working even on Sunday night to locate a missing gas main, so that the sound of the shot would be drowned – Callan told it all, right down to his dislike of silencers: they could throw a bullet out of trajectory – and his detestation of his orders to rifle the dead man's safe.

At last he said, 'You may wonder, Inspector, why Hunter didn't just tell me to run Schneider down in a car? There are two reasons. One – it isn't all that easy, not if you want to make it look like an accident and the operator to get away. But the other is far more important. Hunter wants it *known* that Schneider was murdered. In fairness to him, he'd see no point in it otherwise. That's why he's letting the girl Jenny live. I'm to tell her to get out, and that if she tries to shop me she'll die. She'll believe it all right. After all she'll have seen Schneider's body– And once she's out she'll talk to other gun-runners, and they'll be warned. She doesn't know it, but that's the price Hunter's demanding for her freedom.' He hesitated then for the first time, as he sought an appropriate ending. 'Well, that's it,' he said at last. 'There's nothing more to tell you. Gawd knows what you've got is enough. I hope you never hear this, Inspector – and you too, Sergeant – but if you do, I hope you'll be able to use it. The way things are now – maybe they can stop you – whoever they are. In any case, if you do decide to act on this, good luck to both of you. Believe me – you'll need it.'

He switched off then, and looked at his watch. He'd told the whole thing in seventeen minutes, filled, emptied, refilled the bath. He tested the water's temperature. Perfect. Callan went into his living-room, undressed, then came back to the bath. With him he brought his copy of Oman. There'd be time for a chapter before the water got too cold.

Meres said, I listened for almost half an hour. He did nothing but fill the bath.'

'For half an hour?' said Hunter.

'Seventeen minutes actually, sir. He filled it, emptied it and then filled it again.'

'Why one earth should he do that?'

'He's a rather poor person,' said Meres. 'I mean financially poor. I think he usually washes shirts and things in the bath.'

'I've no doubt you're right,' said Hunter. 'He's a clean sort of man.

Really, Meres thought. The old boy's going ga-ga. Fixated by Callan's bath-water.

'But running water is something I dislike intensely,' said Hunter, 'when we're bugging a place I mean. It blots out every other noise. Dear boy, forgive an old man's over-anxiety, but could Callan have got hold of a tape-recorder?'

Meres said gently, 'He's under round-the-clock surveillance, sir.'

'Not in his office,' said Hunter, 'and that whole office building is full of telephones. And he did meet Lonely tonight.'

'But Lonely didn't give him anything.'

'Lonely bumped into Callan,' Hunter said. 'Dear dear, what an old alarmist I am. But we have a file on Lonely – because of his connection with Callan you understand. I looked it up today – after I'd heard that Callan had gone to see him. Do you know that wretched little man has been to prison ten times? Four of them were for offences described as larceny from the person. In any other language but policeman's legal, that means he's a pickpocket. And according to the evidence he's very good at it.'

Meres said, 'I see.'

'I really believe you do. Perhaps you'd look into it for me would you? Tomorrow? If we left it till Sunday there'd be no time to revise our arrangements.'

Callan slept well that night and made his way to the office on Saturday feeling better than he'd dared hope. The wire-recorder was safe in his pocket, his stomach had settled down, he wasn't late. Everything so far had gone well, and there was no reason why he shouldn't get away with it. Lonely had really done a marvellous job. It was a pity he'd had to fob the little man off with ten quid; even that termer had almost cleaned him out. He stepped out briskly from the tube into the almost deserted City. Only bastards like Waterman made their minions work on Saturday, and the supply of minions was drying up, though there were still plenty of bastards about... Callan slowed down a little. The two clerkly men were tailing him again today, and the pace he was setting was too hot for them.

He walked into his office building and up the stairs. No sign of Waterman. He didn't expect one. He rarely came into the City on Saturdays, and when he did it was at ten forty-five, quarter of an hour before the pubs opened, to have a row with Callan. On other Saturdays he telephoned, usually at twelve twenty-five, just before Callan was due to finish, to make sure he hadn't sneaked out early. Rapidly Callan skimmed through the post, then took out the petty cash box and book. Waterman's assaults on the petty cash were sporadic but ruthless, and Callan had long since learned to set aside an hour every Saturday for sorting it out. Waterman's two hobbies, awful women and gin, were both expensive, and Waterman behaved as though this were Callan's fault. The petty cash book was an old, familiar battleground to both of them.

Before he fought over it that Saturday, Callan took a letter from his pocket. It was addressed to Detective Inspector Pollard, New Scotland Yard, and beneath this Callan had written: 'To be opened in the event of my death. D. Callan.' He had no intention of dying, but the decision might not be his. Both Schneider and Hunter might choose to have some say in that matter. Of the two, Callan knew that Hunter was the far more potent enemy. The problem was where to hide the letter until Monday. Always think of everything, Hunter had told him, and everything included the fact that Hunter might have his office searched. On the other hand it had to be in a place where the police – or even Waterman – could find it and pass it on to Pollard. In the end he put the envelope inside another, addressed to himself, from a firm of tinned-food importers, and filed it with a stack of similar letters. A searcher in a hurry might miss it, but Waterman wouldn't. The tinned food people were behind on delivery... Callan opened the petty cash box and groaned. Awful women and gin were more expensive than ever...

He ate lunch in a City pub ('Only cold on a Saturday dear,' said the barmaid. 'We don't get the demand.) and went home with the warmth of five whiskys inside him, and a bottle in his raincoat pocket. It was very necessary to relax the day before a job, and for relaxation whisky was essential. No nosy Miss Brewis on the stairs, thank God. Miss B. always knew when he'd been drinking, and was always so kind about it, so bloody understanding. Five whiskys notwithstanding, he used his key with care. Nobody had touched the lock, and he grunted in relief, then scowled at what he'd done. He really was back in Hunter's clutches. It had been the same just before he'd left the section. Whenever he was half-drunk he'd acknowledged each sign that he was still alive with some kind of physical action: touching wood, crossing his fingers, even a grunt... He went into the flat, and perhaps it was his dislike of himself that slowed him up, perhaps it was the whisky. But he realized that the kitchen window was open a whole second too late. The sound of the blow on his head was enormous, like thunder, and afterwards there came the lightning; an intensity of whiteness with himself at its centre. He pitched forward through the whiteness, and it shattered. Behind it was a tender and welcoming dark.

It was the drill that woke him. They must have got it from a dentist's. The drill was needle-fine and hurt like hell when they placed it against his head and turned on the power. They used it in the same place on the side of his head in twin bursts, over and over again. Pain pain, the drill said. Pain pain. Pain pain. Pain. Pain. And Callan groaned at what the drill was doing, even though groaning was agony too. Then he opened his eyes to curse the men who were using the drill, and the drill became his telephone ringing, and the sound of the telephone hurt as much as the drill had done. He got to his feet slowly, laboriously and lurched towards the phone, fell and crawled to it on his hands and knees, picked it up. The ringing had stopped. He put the phone back on its cradle, lurched to the toilet and was sick. When his stomach stopped heaving, he went into the kitchen, ran the tap till the water was cold and put his head under it. Slowly the pain muted to an ache, insistent but bearable, like a too tight shoe. Cautiously, he dried his face and head, then looked at himself in the mirror above the sink. A neat, professional job.

Probably a plaited leather cosh. Behind the ear but in the hairline. Not even much of a bruise, considering the force of the blow. Callan looked at his watch. He'd been out for over an hour. The bastard had no need to hit as hard as that, surely? He went back into his living-room and saw without surprise the mangled remains of his wire-recorder. One well-placed shoe-heel, and all that Japanese technology was ruined. They'd found the spare spools too, and jumped on them. Only the Scotch was left. Some whimsical sod had even opened it for him and poured him out a tot. Cautiously, Callan sipped. Warm and benign, it settled on his stomach, then the phone rang again, his hand shook and the whisky spilled. Callan picked up the phone.

'Callan,' he said.

'Charlie would like to speak to you,' she said, and her voice was soft and cool as snow.

'Do I have to?' he asked.

'Don't be absurd,' she said. 'I am putting you through.'

Her voice was just the thing for his head, Callan thought, then Hunter came on.

'Feeling better?' he asked.

'Yeah,' said Callan. 'He didn't hit me in a vital spot.'

'How foolish you are,' said Hunter. 'What made you do it?'

'Please,' said Callan. 'No questions. You know why I did it.'

'I heard it played to me, over the telephone, before it was destroyed. You did it extremely well. But it wouldn't have worked, you know.'

'It was worth trying.'

'No,' said Hunter. 'It wasn't. Not any more. I don't exist, Callan. Nor does the man who hit you. The police would never find us. They wouldn't even be allowed to start looking.'

'I know it,' said Callan.

'And yet you committed this absurdity. What an optimist you are. Did you leave any more little souvenirs?'

'Just a note in my office. I told the bogeys where to find the tape.'

'We've already destroyed that,' said Hunter.

'I should have known.'

'Of course you should. Any more?'

'No,' said Callan.

There was a pause, while Hunter evaluated the chances of Callan's lying.

'Stay at home till tomorrow,' he said at last.

'I'm still doing the job then?' Callan asked.

'Certainly,' said Hunter. 'You're stupid but you're accurate. And anyway I haven't time to set up an alternative scheme.' Callan said nothing. 'Well?'

'All right,' said Callan. 'I'll do it.'

'Of course you will,' said Hunter. 'Phone Charlie when it's over.'

Hunter hung up, and looked at Meres, who had been listening on the ear-piece.

'Toby,' he said. 'Why do you hit so hard? He was out for over an hour.'

'I'm very sorry, sir,' said Meres.

'We both know that's not true,' said Hunter. 'All things considered, I think you'd better go along to Schneider's too. Just in case Callan changes his mind.'

'Why not take Callan off it altogether, sir?' said Meres.

'Oh dear no. That would never do,' Hunter said. 'Who was the young man at the Home Office who took Pollard and Grace away from Schneider?'

'Eltringham, sir. He's a friend of mine.'

'Do you think he could be persuaded to put them on again at–When does Schneider die?'

'Eleven o'clock, sir.'

'At, say, ten fifty-five?'

'Very easily, sir,' said Meres.

'Excellent,' said Hunter. 'Perhaps now you understand why Callan's involvement is essential.'

CHAPTER FOURTEEN

Schneider had fed him well. There'd been whisky before dinner, then asparagus soup, roast chicken, fruit salad and hock. Callan had forced himself to eat, but the hock was dangerous, on top of the whisky. He'd begged off after one glass.

'Too German?' Schneider said. 'But once I *was* German. Indulge my nostalgia, Mr. Callan.'

'Too strong,' said Callan. 'I've got two wars to fight.'

He refused the brandy, but drank the coffee Jenny made. It was good coffee: black and strong. Schneider drank brandy and took the bottle with him to the living-room.

'Our kind of war is an aesthetic experience,' Schneider said. 'So is Jenny here. So is brandy. At my age, Mr. Callan, it is foolish to refuse an aesthetic experience.'

'You're talking too much,' said Jenny, but she looked happy.

'As always,' said Schneider. 'Shall we toss for choice of battles, Mr. Callan?'

Jenny spun a coin, and Callan called and lost.

Schneider said, 'Talavera, Mr. Callan. Does it surprise you?'

'Yes,' said Callan. 'You said it was a mess.'

'I choose the French side,' Schneider said. 'That surprises you also?'

'Very much.'

'I have had a theory about Talavera for seven years. If it is sound, Talavera will be a mess no longer.'

So it was Spain, in the hot, dusty summer of 1809, and Callan was Sir Arthur Wellesley, the cold and imperturbable Irishman commanding England's last army, phlegmatic redcoats, overenthusiastic cavalry, with his best troops and artillery fifty miles away; and in their place his Spanish allies, infrequently fed and even less frequently paid, commanded by the septuagenarian Don Gregorio de la Cuesta, who looked back on a record of unbroken defeat. These were Callan's forces.

Against him Schneider mustered an army of forty thousand Frenchmen (twice the strength of the British force): a veteran army that accepted victory as its inevitable due; strong in cavalry and artillery, skilful and courageous, their titular head King Joseph,

Napoleon's brother, but their real leader Marshal Jourdan, shrewd and determined, picked by Napoleon himself. The British occupied the green hills that shouldered their way towards Talavera: the Spaniards roamed the area with a volatility compounded equally of optimism and ignorance; stumbling on to the French, retreating, regrouping, while their elderly commander slept, but somehow managing to avoid the action that came, first by night, then throughout a day of heat so intense that both sides called impromptu truces and drank from the stagnant pools of an almost dried up stream. At the end of a muddled and uncertain battle King Joseph and Jourdan retreated. Wellesley wrote dispatches, and de la Cuesta went back to sleep.

So it had been in reality, but Schneider, facing Callan across the great table, had other plans. Unlike Jourdan, he launched his attack at the Spaniards, hoping to embroil the British infantry in their protection. His attack was a complete success, the Spaniards were routed, but Callan refused to commit a man. Instead, he entrenched his army among the hills, and held out against the wearying French as time went by and his reinforcements drew nearer and nearer at the Light Brigade quickstep of three paces at a walk followed by three paces at a run. Schneider moved his hands towards a French division massed in column.

'You are a heartless commander. Mr. Callan,' he said. 'Your allies are all dead.'

'My men are alive,' Callan said.

Schneider said, 'This young man has forced me to see the truth.'

'It won't last,' said Jenny.

'You're teasing me,' Schneider said. 'That is good. I like it. Come.'

She walked over to him at once, and Schneider put an arm round her shoulders, then marched her to the middle of the table.

'Look,' he said. 'Here is Sir Arthur Wellesley's army. Here is Sir Arthur Wellesley.' He nodded at Callan. 'Within five years he will be a duke – the first Duke of Wellington.'

'Congratulations,' said Jenny.

'See how pale he is on the eve of victory,' said Schneider.

'I'm sorry. I think I'm starting a cold,' said Callan.

Schneider went on unheeding.

'I am a marshal of France, Jourdan, friend of Napoleon, military expert, child of the revolution. It is my good fortune to obliterate the one remaining British army, and make my emperor master of Europe. I have courage, skill and an overwhelming number of first-rate troops. But I am also a fool. I fail to see the obvious.'

'It doesn't sound like you,' said Jenny.

'Now we talk of war, my love,' said Schneider. 'In love, Jourdan was different also. My foolishness is this. I fail to see that if Wellesley disposes his troops as he has done, then stands by while his allies are cut to pieces, I cannot win. I gamble on Wellesley's sense of the English fair play, and overlook the fact that Wellesley is Irish. Fair play means no more to him than it does to me. So I gamble, and I lose. It is inevitable. I cannot win. Not even a hundred and sixty years later. I am brilliant in my way– I admit it–'

'I thought you were a fool,' said Jenny.

'As you grow older you will learn that the two are not incompatible. Please don't interrupt. I am brilliant, but Wellesley is a genius.' He bowed to Callan.

'He goes on like this all the time,' Jenny said. 'You'll get used to it.'

'Not when he's fighting,' said Callan.

'That's because he likes to win,' said Jenny.

Callan said, 'That's what I like about him.'

Schneider said, 'Please don't talk as if you were writing my obituary.'

Jenny laughed, a clear, ringing sound of joy.

'You won't die,' she said. 'Not ever.'

And Callan stood by and watched, as Schneider kissed his girl. He felt nothing. There was nothing to feel: only the battle to come, and Schneider's death at eleven o'clock precisely.

'Mr. Callan really beat you?' Jenny asked.

'He really did,' said Schneider.

'I didn't know anyone could stop Rudi,' Jenny said, and looked unsmiling at Callan. 'You must be good,' she said.

'Thanks,' said Callan.

Schneider poured more brandy.

'Which battle do you choose?' he asked.

'Gettysburg,' Callan said. 'I'll leave you the choice of generals.'

'In which case you will lose,' said Schneider. 'I shall be Robert E. Lee.' He began to put away the Peninsular soldiers, and extracted from the chest the Federal army in blue, the Confederate army in grey. As he did so, the first blast of pneumatic drills outside the house exploded like heavy machine guns. Schneider swore vilely in German and strode to the door.

'Did Robert E. Lee really win this battle?' Jenny asked.

'No,' said Callan. 'Nothing went right for him.'

'And the other commander? The one you will be?'

'Meade? He was a middle-aged man, bad-tempered and cautious. The two don't usually go together.'

'Was he a genius, too?'

'No,' said Callan. 'Meade was very competent, but Lee was the genius.'

'I'm glad,' said Jenny.

Schneider erupted back into the room, his eyes glittering with ill-temper.

'Sunday night is no time to repair a gas-main,' he said. 'Is this what I pay my rates for?' Suddenly his eyes grew mild, and he shouted with laughter. 'How very British I am,' he said, and turned to Callan. 'Wouldn't you say I'm British?'

'Oh, extremely,' said Callan, 'except that at the moment you're a very gallant gentleman from Virginia.'

'Lee,' said Schneider. 'He was almost too much of a good thing, wasn't he? Gallant, brilliant, honourable. He *deserved* to win at Gettysburg. Tonight he shall.'

Outside, the pneumatic drills sounded the opening salvos of a nation's agony.

Meres' first task had been to immobilize George. It hadn't been difficult. He'd simply waited until George came back from his nightly trip to the pub (two cautious pints), taken shelter by the door of the garage-flat, then coshed George as he opened the door. George had taken no precautions: there was no reason why he should expect to be coshed. After all, the door to his flat was under observation by three witnesses – the men who were digging up the road. He made a very easy target, and Meres hit it with controlled skill as the road gang continued with their business of supplying background noise. Meres dragged George up the stairs – Christ he was heavy! – laid him on the bed and gave him an injection – enough for an hour – then produced a half-bottle of whisky, poured some over George's shirt and a little into his mouth, swallowed some himself then poured most of the rest down the sink. He switched on a transistor radio, kicked over a chair, then pressed the half-bottle into George's right hand and let it fall to the floor. What pigs servants were. They didn't even use glasses. Meres looked at his watch. It was ten forty-five.

Gettysburg was another summer battle. As June ended, Lee had taken his army across the Potomac, and wheeled east into Pennsylvania. It was a splendid army, the Army of Northern Virginia, brave, professional and ably led, but it was an army of infantry and artillery only. The cavalry, led by Jeb Stuart, had achieved a feat as brilliant as it was futile: ridden round the entire Union Army. It was a feat that took ten days, and Stuart failed to rejoin Lee till the battle was more than half over, and without cavalry, Lee was fighting blind. Meade's army advanced to meet him, and the two sides stumbled on each other at Gettysburg. In the fighting of the first day the Union troops were heavily outnumbered and soundly beaten, but Meade was a brave and obstinate man, and hung on while Lee attacked, for two long, agonizing days. The culmination of Lee's assault was an attack of a whole division, fifteen thousand men, on the Union army's central position at Cemetery Ridge. It was an assault that almost succeeded, but in war, almost is never good enough. The attacking column broke and fell back after appalling loss, and the Battle of Gettysburg was over. Lee's army had lost twenty thousand men, a third of its numbers. The North had taken even more casualties, but it was Lee who was forced to retreat, back to Virginia, back to the South...

Callan waited as Schneider addressed himself to Lee's problems, smoothed them and simplified them with the knowledge that hindsight brings: keeping a tighter hold on Stuart, massing his artillery more advantageously, probing with scouts and horsemen before undertaking the enormous gamble of Pickett's charge. But the trouble was that hindsight works two ways, and Callan too had done his research, read what the authorities had to say about improving Meade's defence in depth. Five to eleven. Two minutes to. Time for Schneider to die. But maybe it would be wiser to wait a while: to see if Jenny went to bed: kinder too, for Jenny and for Schneider, to let him finish the battle first. To let him win? No. Schneider asked for no man's charity.

He set himself to counter Schneider's moves. As in Talavera, his rôle was defensive. Only in reality would he go on to the attack. Schneider in this battle was bold, ruthless, brilliant. Callan imagined the battle as he struggled to counter Schneider; the bellow of cannon, the rebel yells, the patter of Minie balls, then more and more insistently, the groans and screams of the wounded. Over forty thousand men in three days, dead, or seriously wounded, or missing. Callan dug into the hills and hung on.

Jenny said, 'Rudi!' Then more loudly, 'Rudi! Darling!'

For the only time in their lives together, Schneider looked at her as at a stranger. He was sweating, obsessed with the battle, and Callan had no doubt that he looked like that too. At last recognition came into Schneider's eyes.

'I'm sorry, Liebchen,' he said. 'Even Robert E. Lee has his problems. What is it?'

'There are two men to see you,' Jenny said. 'A Mr. Pollard and a Mr. Grace.'

'It's very inconvenient,' Schneider said. 'Pickett's division is about to charge. The South is going to win the war.'

'Maybe,' said Callan.

'They asked me to say it's urgent,' said Jenny.

Schneider said, 'It must be. It's a quarter past eleven.' He bowed to Callan. 'Excuse me, please,' he said.

'Of course,' said Callan.

'I trust you,' Schneider said, and wagged a forefinger. 'No cheating.'

Meres had seen the police arrive. But

there'd been no shot, he was sure of it, even with those bloody drills thumping away. Hunter was right as usual; it was just as well he'd had Meres on hand. It was time for him to break into Schneider's house. The kitchen window was the easy one. All it took was a rubber sucker and a diamond cutter, then open the latch, cut the burglar alarm and step over the sink. Out of the kitchen then, and into the study. That was next to the drawing-room: the battlefield. When Schneider got rid of the police he'd walk right in on him, and Callan could watch. Maybe he'd learn something.

CHAPTER FIFTEEN

'It looks very complicated,' Jenny was saying. 'Will Rudi win?'

'He can't,' Callan said.

'Why not?'

'Well you see,' said Callan, 'my infantry are–' He paused and looked at her. She was listening far too intently. 'No, ma'am,' said Callan. 'I recognize a beautiful Confederate spy when I see one. I'll tell you after the battle.'

'I don't think so,' she said. 'I'm going to bed.' She was angry with him.

'It's only a game you know,' Callan said gently. 'They play it at staff colleges. You learn to be Wellington – or Robert E. Lee.'

'Were *you* at staff college?' she asked.

'No.'

'Rudi was at Potsdam. They said he was brilliant. When the war ended–'

'It's better with models. They don't bleed,' Callan said.

Meres grimaced as he listened at the door.

'Rudi agrees with you now,' said Jenny,

then tried once more. 'Please, Mr. Callan, can't you let him win?' she asked. 'Winning's important to him.'

'It's important to both of us,' said Callan. She gave up then.

'Excuse me,' she said. 'I must fetch a book from the study. Then I'll leave you to your war.' She was mad at him again: she really must adore Schneider.

'I wish you a very good night,' she said. She didn't mean it.

She went into the study and Callan heard the thud almost at once. He leaped for the door and pushed it open. Jenny lay sprawled on the floor, all legs and flowing hair, as Meres bent over her. He looked up. There was a gun in his hand. Callan didn't think it quite steady enough.

'Get on with it, Callan,' he said.

'You must be joking,' said Callan. 'Schneider's got two rozzers with him. Tell Hunter the deal's off.'

'He won't like that,' said Meres.

'I'll find time to cry about it. Look, mate – if I'd shot Schneider on time I'd have been nicked – and Hunter knew it.'

Meres said only, 'He has to die.'

Callan looked at the gun in Meres' hand. It trembled only slightly, but it was enough.

'All right,' he said. 'Just let's wait till the fuzz goes away.'

He left the study and very quickly locked its door, pocketed the key, then went across the living-room to the other door that led to the hall, and listened. Schneider was saying, 'We've been through all this before, gentlemen. It's late and I have a guest.'

'Mind telling us his name, sir?'

There was a pause, and Callan found that the palms of his hands were wet.

'Yes I do mind,' said Schneider. 'Nor did I say it was a man. Please go.'

Callan went back to the study door and whispered. 'He's coming back. Get out of here you bloody fool.'

There was no answer, only a tiny sound of metal on metal. The idiot was trying to unscrew the lock from the door. Callan went back to the table and was absorbed in Gettysburg when Schneider came in.

'Where's Jenny?' he asked at once.

'She's gone to bed,' said Callan, and Schneider grinned.

'Wars make Jenny unhappy,' he said. 'Even our wars. She is very female.'

'She is indeed,' said Callan. 'You're a lucky man.'

Schneider looked down on Gettysburg.

'In love, certainly,' he said. 'In war I am not so sure.'

He pushed a mass of grey-clad infantry slowly forward, like a gambler betting all his chips on one number.

'What a clever young man you are,' he said. 'You leave me no choice. Your whole battle-plan has brought me to this point – is it not so? If I don't risk everything, I am lost anyway. And so I must gamble Pickett's division, fifteen thousand men – and take that hill.'

'You can't,' said Callan. 'You've left it too late – just as Lee did. My artillery's massed. Look at it.'

Old-fashioned muzzle-loaders. But at the time there had been nothing quaint about them.

'The infantry dug rifle-pits. They had sharp-shooters under cover,' said Callan. 'And the cavalry are fresh. Not like yours, worn out after a ten days' ride. Pickett's division was chopped to bits. It will be again.'

Schneider looked again, and sighed.

'In fact, we shall never know,' he said. 'Fifteen thousand heroes – what could they not do? But by all the logic of war you are right. The attack must fail – on paper. But I can do something that Lee could not.' He pulled back the grey-clad infantry and turned them round towards the Potomac and Virginia. 'I can withdraw,' said Schneider. 'The field of honour is yours.'

He smiled again, that infectious, brilliant smile that turned even defeat into a pleasure.

'You are a very clever young man,' he said again. 'You were never trained at Potsdam and I was – and yet you beat me. But cleverness is not everything, Mr. Callan. You are also – forgive me – a cold man. You show it in the way you fight.'

'And an unsuccessful one,' Callan said.

'With your intelligence it cannot last. Come. Let me give you a drink.'

'If you don't mind,' said Callan. 'It's late. And I've got this cold coming.'

'As you wish,' Schneider said. 'Please do whatever you like.'

So I'm leaving him to Meres, Callan thought. I'm glad, Schneider old love. I never wanted to kill you, and after tonight I don't think I could anyway.

Again there came the clink of metal from the study. Callan willed himself not to look at the lock. Schneider it seemed hadn't heard the sound.

'Before you go, let me show you one more

of my treasures, Mr. Callan,' he said, and walked to the chest of soldiers. As Callan moved forward, Schneider opened the chest, pulled out a drawer and produced a gun: a modern nine-millimetre Walther semi-automatic. It was fully loaded, and aimed at Callan's heart.

Schneider said loudly, 'Is it not magnificent?'

His voice drowned Callan's yelp of frightened, conventional protest. He moved up to Callan.

'Be still,' he whispered, and his hands moved deftly over Callan's body, seeking a gun. He found none.

'Forgive me,' Schneider whispered. 'But someone has broken into my study. I hope you are not involved – but make no sound.' He pushed Callan behind a chair. 'Make a sound or try to escape – and I will kill you.'

He backed off then, moving to the study door.

'Let me persuade you to change your mind,' he said aloud. 'Just one more battle. Armageddon.' As he spoke he whirled, his foot drew back and he kicked open the door. The impact knocked Meres to the floor, and Schneider looked down on him, and Jenny. Meres' gun lay by the door. Schneider picked it up left-handed.

'You must hope that you haven't killed her,' he said.

His back was to Callan, and it gave him the time he needed. He pulled up his right trouser-leg. The Noguchi lay along the inside of his calf, butt upwards, held in place by a strip of adhesive tape padded with cotton wool. Callan drew it out and stuck it in his waistband. He had no wish to interfere, but the gun was a comfort.

Meres said, 'She's unconscious, that's all.'

'It may be you will think her fortunate,' said Schneider, and put Meres' gun in his pocket. 'Come.' He waved the Walther, and Meres got up and went into the living-room. Callan looked at him blankly, and Schneider said, 'You do not know this man?'

'Of course not,' said Callan.

Meres said, 'Come off it. It was your job to keep him busy while I broke in.'

So I'm committed after all, Callan thought.

'So,' said Schneider. 'You are not so unsuccessful after all. But why no gun, Mr. Callan?'

'My mate's the heavy,' Callan said.

'Not burglars. Definitely not burglars,' Schneider said aloud. 'But I think you would have opened my safe – and made a noise. I would have come down, and you would have killed me. Is that the story?'

Meres said nothing.

'But your police were on to me. They came here tonight. Didn't your chief know that?' Schneider said.

'Of course,' said Meres. 'But they had no proof of what you do.'

'And you have proof?'

'We know,' Meres said. 'That's why you're going to die.'

'Perhaps,' said Schneider. 'If your people can find me.' He half-turned to Callan. 'This man means nothing to me – but you – I liked you. You may have your choice. Who shall die first?'

'Him,' said Callan, and Meres grimaced.

'Of course,' said Schneider. 'Even a few seconds more is better than nothing. I'm sorry.'

He waited till the pneumatic drill began a new burst, then swung round on Meres. As he did so, Callan's hand stabbed down, came up with the Noguchi, and the gun was a pointing finger. He fired once, an appalling outrage of sound in a closed room, and Schneider fell as if he had been thrown.

'Me too,' said Callan.

He walked over and looked down at the body. Through the back of the head. There was no need for a second shot.

'You took your bloody time,' said Meres. 'Let's get out of here.'

'I'm supposed to rob the safe,' said Callan.

'Then for God's sake be quick.'

'Go and get rid of that noise, then give me a hand,' said Callan.

Meres went to the front door and signalled to the workmen as Callan opened Schneider's safe with the key he had made. When Meres came back, the wads of money lay ready for the taking. 'Christ,' said Meres, and went towards them.

'Just a minute,' said Callan. 'Were you the geezer who coshed me?'

'As a matter of fact I was,' said Meres. 'Sorry about that – Hunter's orders.' He turned back to the safe. 'No hard feelings, old boy.'

Callan hit him behind the ear with the butt of the Noguchi, then stood back as he fell.

'No hard feelings,' said Callan.

He wiped the Noguchi then, and pressed it into Meres' hand. That left him without a gun. He went over to Schneider and took Meres' gun from Schneider's pocket. The gaiety, the zest for life, was gone from Schneider now. There was a sound at the study door and Callan swung round behind the gun-barrel's rigid accusation. Jenny stood, clinging to the doorway, swaying, her face all eyes that stared at Schneider's body.

'He's dead,' said Callan. 'He smuggled guns for money and now he's dead.'

'You killed him?' Jenny asked.

'Yes,' said Callan.

Wearily she said, 'That's three times you beat him. I should have known.' She looked at Meres. 'And this man – did he help you?'

'He thought so,' Callan said. 'But he just got in the way.'

Jenny lurched into the room, moving towards Schneider, but Callan intercepted her, blocking her off from the body. 'I shouldn't,' he said.

He took her arm and led her to the safe. She made no resistance.

'You're doing yourself no good here, love,' he said. 'You'd better start running.' He took a wad of money from the safe and pressed it into her hand.

'Take this,' he said, 'and scarper.'

'I hate you,' Jenny said, her voice a whisper. 'I hate you, Callan. If I could kill you I would.'

'All right,' said Callan. 'I'll remember. Now get.'

She left then, clutching the money, and Callan thought it would be as well not to forget the look in her eyes. Quickly he wiped off the things he had touched, the soldiers, cannon, the glass he had drunk from, went into the kitchen and looked for his glass and plates. They were all washed, and carefully dried. Housewifely, deadly Jenny. He went back into the living-room, wrapped a handkerchief round the whisky decanter and swigged it down. Good stuff. Chivas Regal. The same that Hunter had offered him when he got into this mess. He put the decanter down and looked at the table. The Confederates were still in retreat when he left. He slammed the front door behind him and looked at the deserted hole in the road. It was the size and shape of a grave.

On the way up the road, he thought of the price of what had been done: of what *he* had done. Arthur, dead: the Greek, Papadopoulos, drugged out of his mind: Lonely, scared out of his: Jenny, planning the death of Callan, even as she ran. And Meres, good old Toby, about to wake up to a murder charge. He wished Hunter could wake up to one too, and went into the phone booth.

'Yes?' said the voice, cool and exquisite as always.

I shall never see her again, thought Callan.

'This is Callan,' he said. 'Let me speak to Charlie.'

Hunter came on at once.

'I'm here,' he said.

The bastard's worried, Callan thought. Congratulations, Callan.

'Our friend passed away,' he said. 'Quite suddenly. At home – after the police left.'

'Ah,' said Hunter. 'I'm sorry about that.'

'You should be,' said Callan. 'They'll be back in a minute, and that old Etonian Capone's still in the house.'

There was a pause. Callan hoped that Hunter was sweating.

'Can't you get him out?' he asked at last.

'Of course I can,' said Callan.

'Fine,' said Hunter. 'Go and collect him. Bring him back here. I think he'd better work under you for a bit. It seems he has a lot to learn.'

Callan took his time about it.

'No,' he said.

'Oh, come now, Callan, he merely obeyed orders,' said Hunter.

'I mean, No I won't get him out. I'm not going to work for you, Hunter. Not ever.'

He banged the phone down, then dialled 9-9-9.

The calm, metallic voice said, 'Emergency. Which service do you require?'

'Police,' said Callan.

Hunter looked at the phone in his hand then replaced it carefully. Callan had never dared hang up on him before, but there simply wasn't time to be angry. He pressed the key of his Dictaphone.

'Yes, sir?' she said.

'Have you got Callan's file there?' he asked.

'One moment, sir,' she said, then, 'Yes. It's here, sir.'

'It's in a yellow cover, isn't it?'

'Yes, sir. Yellow.'

Hunter sighed. The desire for rage had gone. Now there was only regret.

'Change that for a red one please,' he said.

The publishers hope that this book has given you enjoyable reading. Large Print Books are especially designed to be as easy to see and hold as possible. If you wish a complete list of our books please ask at your local library or write directly to:

Magna Large Print Books
Magna House, Long Preston,
Skipton, North Yorkshire.
BD23 4ND

This Large Print Book, for people
who cannot read normal print,
is published under the auspices of

THE ULVERSCROFT FOUNDATION

... we hope you have enjoyed this book.
Please think for a moment about those
who have worse eyesight than you ...
and are unable to even read or enjoy
Large Print without great difficulty.

You can help them by sending a
donation, large or small, to:

**The Ulverscroft Foundation,
1, The Green, Bradgate Road,
Anstey, Leicestershire, LE7 7FU,
England.**
or request a copy of our brochure for
more details.

The Foundation will use all donations
to assist those people who are visually
impaired and need special attention
with medical research, diagnosis
and treatment.

Thank you very much for your help.